白
松

THE FALLEN
KŌKEN

後見

BY

N. K. EDO

Prologue

THE TALE OF KŌKEN TAKASHI

LONG AGO, IN THE days when the Kōken were revered across the land as protectors and guides, there was a warrior known as Takashi, whose skill with a blade was unmatched. Takashi was a man of great potential, chosen from a young age to be trained in the ancient ways of the Kōken. His master, a stern and wise old Kōken, saw in him a fire that could either light the way for others or consume him entirely.

For years, Takashi trained under the strict guidance of his master. He learned the art of combat, the discipline of mind, and the importance of humility. Takashi was ambitious, eager to prove himself, and his talents grew with each passing day. Yet, beneath his skill and strength lay a deep hunger—not just for victory, but for recognition, power, and the rewards that came with them.

When Takashi's training was complete, his master sent him out into the world to serve as a Kōken. He was tasked with protecting the weak, guiding the lost, and defending the land from the forces of darkness. For a time, Takashi was faithful to his duties, and his name became known far and wide.

But as Takashi's fame grew, so did his desire for more. The villagers he protected showered him with gifts, food, and wealth, grateful for his protection. Takashi, who had once lived a life of modesty and discipline, began to indulge in these offerings. The simple life of a Kōken no longer satisfied him; he craved luxury and power.

One day, Takashi arrived in a prosperous town beset by a monstrous oni. The creature had terrorized the people, leaving destruction in its wake. The townsfolk, desperate for salvation, pleaded with Takashi to save them. In exchange, they promised him riches beyond his wildest dreams and a place of honor among them.

Takashi accepted the offer, and with his incredible skill, he defeated the oni in a fierce battle. The town was saved, and true to their word, the people rewarded Takashi handsomely. But the victory did not bring him peace; instead, it only fueled his greed.

Takashi remained in the town, accepting tributes from the people who had once revered him as a hero. His once noble heart grew cold, and he became a tyrant, using his power to control and oppress the very people he had sworn to protect. He justified his actions by telling himself that the world was harsh and that only through his control could the town survive.

The other Kōken, hearing of Takashi's fall from grace, sent word that he must return to the path or face judgment. But Takashi, now fully consumed by his desires, ignored their warnings. He believed himself invincible, beyond the reach of those who once called him brother.

It was then that the Kōken who had trained Takashi appeared before him, his face lined with sorrow. The old master pleaded with his former student to remember the teachings of their order, to return to the way of the Kōken before it was too late. But Takashi, blinded by his greed, laughed at his master's words and challenged him.

The battle between master and student was fierce, each strike filled with the weight of their shared past. But in the end, it was the master who emerged victorious, his heart heavy with regret as he dealt the final blow.

As Takashi lay dying, the light fading from his eyes, he finally understood the price of his ambition. His master knelt beside him, whispering a final lesson—a lesson that Takashi had been too blind to see until it was too late.

"Power," the master said, "is not the measure of a Kōken. It is the burden we carry. The true strength of a Kōken lies not in dominance, but in service. And those who forget this lesson are destined to fall."

Takashi's story became a warning to all Kōken—a tale of a warrior who fell victim to his own greed, who lost his way and paid the ultimate price. It is said that his spirit still wanders the land, a restless ghost searching for the peace that eluded him in life.

THE AIR AROUND THEM felt electric, charged with an unseen force as Wakamono faced the kyonshii. The creature stood hunched over, its pallid skin stretched tight across sinewy muscle. Glowing, malevolent red eyes locked onto Wakamono, its mouth hanging open to reveal jagged, decaying teeth. The air around it was cold, as if its very presence drained warmth from the forest.

Wakamono shifted his stance, gripping the hilt of his katana tightly. He could feel his heartbeat in his fingertips, a steady thrum of adrenaline coursing through him. Red Mist stood a few paces back, her arms folded, observing. This was his fight.

Without warning, the kyonshii moved. Its unnatural speed was startling, and Wakamono barely had time to bring his katana up to block the initial strike. The creature's claws met the blade with a high-pitched screech, sparks flying as they scraped against the steel. Wakamono pushed back, using the momentum to shove the kyonshii away and give himself some breathing room.

But the kyonshii wasn't done. It launched itself at him again, its feet barely touching the ground as it pounced. Wakamono sidestepped, his movements swift, his katana flashing out in a horizontal arc. The blade sliced through the kyonshii's ragged robes, but the creature twisted in mid-air, avoiding the full brunt of the attack.

Wakamono gritted his teeth and spun, bringing the katana up in a tight arc, aiming for the creature's neck. This time, the blade connected. Blood—or whatever ichor passed for it—splattered across the ground as the kyonshii let out a screech of rage. The wound wasn't fatal, but Wakamono had drawn first blood.

"Good," Red Mist called out from the edge of the clearing. "Keep your focus. Don't give it an opening."

Wakamono nodded, his gaze never leaving the kyonshii. The creature hissed at him, its movements growing more erratic, more desperate. It lashed out again, and Wakamono met the attack head-on. He blocked the swipe aimed at his head, then countered with a quick thrust directed toward the creature's chest.

But the kyonshii was quick. It twisted out of the way, using the momentum to swing its claws in a vicious backhand aimed at Wakamono's midsection.

The blow connected before Wakamono could react, sending him stumbling back.

He gasped for air, his vision swimming as he tried to steady himself. The kyonshii lunged forward, sensing weakness. Its claws came down in a savage arc, aimed directly at Wakamono's exposed throat.

Time seemed to slow as Wakamono raised his katana, bracing himself for the impact. He barely managed to block the strike, but the force behind it was immense. His knees buckled under the weight, and the blade slipped in his grip, sending a jolt of pain up his arms. Dark fluid oozed from the kyonshii's flesh where it gripped the blade.

The kyonshii snarled, pressing down harder, its glowing eyes full of murderous intent. Wakamono's muscles screamed in protest as he fought to keep the blade from giving way. Sweat dripped down his brow, his heart hammering in his chest.

In a split-second decision, Wakamono pivoted, allowing the blade to slide out from under the kyonshii's claws. The sudden shift caused the creature to stumble, its balance thrown off just enough for Wakamono to roll out of the way.

Wakamono came up on one knee, his katana ready, but the kyonshii was already charging again. It was relentless, a whirlwind of claws and snarls, and Wakamono was forced onto the defensive, barely able to keep up with the onslaught. He blocked a strike aimed at his face, then ducked under another that would have torn his shoulder open.

He was growing tired. His arms ached, his movements slowing. The kyonshii could sense it too. It let out a screech of triumph, its claws flashing toward Wakamono's chest in a final, deadly strike.

Wakamono's instincts kicked in, and he twisted his body, bringing the katana up just in time to block the attack. But the force of the blow was too much. The impact sent Wakamono sprawling, his back hitting the ground hard. He gasped in pain, the wind knocked from his lungs.

The kyonshii loomed over him, its claws raised high, ready to deliver the killing blow. Wakamono's heart pounded in his ears as he struggled to raise his katana. His arms felt like lead, his vision blurring.

And then, in a flash of steel, the kyonshii's hand was severed at the wrist.

Red Mist moved like a shadow, her katana slicing through the air with deadly precision. Before the kyonshii could react, she spun, her blade flashing out again, severing its head in one fluid motion. The creature's body crumpled to the ground, disintegrating into ash.

Wakamono lay there for a moment, breathing heavily, the adrenaline still coursing through him. Red Mist stood over him, her expression unreadable as she wiped her blade clean.

"You fought well," she said, her voice calm. "But you let the fight drag on too long. You need to be faster. More decisive."

Wakamono groaned as he pushed himself to his feet, wiping the blood from his lip. "I had it... under control," he muttered, though he knew it wasn't true.

Red Mist raised an eyebrow. "Did you?"

Wakamono didn't respond. He couldn't meet her eyes. He had been reckless, letting the fight drag on too long. He had let the kyonshii gain the upper hand, and it had almost cost him his life.

Red Mist placed a hand on his shoulder, her touch light but firm. "You're growing stronger, Wakamono. But strength alone isn't enough. You need self-control. Patience. Discipline."

He nodded, his gaze fixed on the ground. "I'll do better next time."

Red Mist nodded once, her expression softening slightly. "I know you will."

後見

The marketplace was alive with energy, the air thick with the scent of fresh fruits, grilled meats, and baked bread. The sun hung high overhead, casting a golden glow over the bustling streets. Merchants shouted their wares from colorful stalls, their voices blending with the laughter of children and the chatter of townsfolk. The clinking of coins echoed through the air as trades were made, and the rhythmic clatter of wooden wheels rolling over cobblestone streets added to the music of the market.

Wakamono's senses were alight, his eyes scanning the array of foods and goods on display. Brightly colored silks waved gently in the breeze, their hues as vibrant as the flowers sold at a nearby stand. A woman hawked baskets of persimmons, while a man at a stall roasted chestnuts over an open fire. The aroma made Wakamono's stomach rumble, reminding him of how hungry he was after the battle with the kyonshii.

Despite the earlier danger, there was a certain calmness that washed over him now. The marketplace was peaceful, full of life and warmth. It felt good to be in the thick of it, where life carried on without the constant threat of battle. He allowed himself to relax, if only for a moment.

"Red Mist," he began, his voice light, "what do you think of grabbing something to eat? I've been dreaming of those grilled sweet potatoes since the last time we were here."

Red Mist walked beside him, her gaze scanning the crowd with practiced calm. Her posture was as sharp as ever, but there was a rare softness in her expression, a fleeting sense of satisfaction. She hadn't said much since they left the clearing where the kyonshii had met its end, but Wakamono could feel her silent approval.

"Sweet potatoes?" she asked, a faint smile tugging at the corner of her lips. "You think of food even after a battle with that disgusting creature?"

Wakamono grinned, his eyes lighting up. "After a battle's the best time for a feast, right?"

Red Mist shook her head, her smile fading as her attention was pulled to a nearby conversation.

In the corner of the market, a group of merchants had gathered, their voices hushed but urgent. Wakamono noticed the tension in Red Mist's stance, her body stilling as she listened to their words. He followed her lead, his curiosity piqued.

"He's demanding more now," one of the merchants muttered, his brow furrowed with worry. "Said the crops weren't enough this season. Now it's gold. How are we supposed to keep up?"

Another merchant, a woman with lines of worry etched across her face, whispered back, "If we don't pay, we know what'll happen. The last family that didn't… well, we all saw what he did."

A third voice joined in, softer, almost reverent. "They say he's unstoppable. That no one can stand against him. A Kōken with power like that? We're at his mercy."

"That's why I don't do business in Hanamachi anymore. Shiro is a threat to us all."

The name that fell from the woman's lips was barely audible, but it hit Wakamono like a stone. *Shiro*.

He felt the shift in Red Mist immediately. Her body, once relaxed and at ease, went rigid, her eyes narrowing in a way that made Wakamono's stomach churn. He turned to face her, confusion flickering in his expression.

"Shiro?" he asked. "Who is Shiro?"

For a moment, Red Mist didn't answer. Her gaze was locked on the merchants, but it was distant, as though she were no longer in the present. Memories seemed to flood her mind, memories Wakamono wasn't privy to.

"He is or... was a Kōken," she finally said, her voice low, her words measured. "He trained with me. We were... apprentices, together."

The way she said it, Wakamono could feel the weight of her words. There was history there, deep and tangled, like the roots of an old tree.

"Was?" Wakamono pressed gently. "What happened to him?"

There was a hesitation in her response that Wakamono hadn't noticed before, a flicker of uncertainty. Red Mist, his unshakable mentor, seemed taken aback by what she had overheard. It was unsettling.

Red Mist turned to him, her expression hardening. "I don't know, yet," she admitted, her tone firmer now. "But we need to find out."

She stepped forward, her gaze set on the path ahead, her usual calm demeanor masking the turmoil beneath. Wakamono hesitated for a moment, trying to make sense of what he had just heard. Shiro—a name he had never known, yet it seemed to carry so much weight for Red Mist.

"Do you think he's... dangerous?" Wakamono asked as he fell into step beside her.

Red Mist didn't answer immediately, her eyes scanning the busy streets as if she were searching for something, or someone. "Shiro was once like me," she finally said. "But if what those merchants said is true... he may not be the man I once knew."

Wakamono felt a pit of unease forming in his stomach. This was the first time he had seen Red Mist look truly uncertain.

"Whatever he's become, we'll find out soon enough," Red Mist continued. "We're going to that town. We need to see for ourselves."

The sounds of the marketplace continued to hum around them, but for Wakamono, the noise faded into the background. The mention of Shiro had shifted the atmosphere entirely, and the weight of whatever history lay between Red Mist and her old comrade was now heavy on his shoulders.

He followed Red Mist through the crowd, but his mind was buzzing with questions.

後見

As they returned to the quiet safety of their residence, the energy of the marketplace behind them, the weight of the new mission hung between Red Mist and Wakamono like an unspoken word. Wakamono could still feel the tension from earlier when the name Shiro had slipped into the conversation of the merchants. His mind was spinning, trying to make sense of the vague pieces of history Red Mist had shared, but he knew better than to press her further—at least for now.

In the dimly lit room, Red Mist was already gathering supplies. She moved quickly and methodically, her hands working with the precision of someone who had done this many times before. Her katana rested against the wall, gleaming faintly in the pale light, as if waiting patiently for its next mission.

"We leave at first light," Red Mist said without turning to face him. Her voice was calm but carried a new, sharper edge—one that Wakamono hadn't heard before. "We'll take the shortcut through the mountains."

Wakamono straightened up, his focus immediately drawn to her words. "The shortcut?" he asked, surprise flickering across his face. "I thought the mountain path was too dangerous. You said merchants avoid it because of the spirits and beasts that roam there."

Red Mist paused, her back still to him as she considered her response. Finally, she turned, meeting his gaze with steady, unwavering eyes. "It is dangerous," she admitted. "But it's also the quickest way to reach the town. If we take the main road, we'll be delayed by two days, maybe more. Time we can't afford to waste."

Wakamono felt a shiver run down his spine. The thought of traversing a path known for its dangers didn't exactly sit comfortably with him, but he trusted Red Mist implicitly. She had faced countless beasts and survived—he had no doubt that she knew what she was doing. Still, the idea of spirits lurking in the shadows of the mountains sent a chill through him.

"What kind of dangers?" he asked, keeping his voice steady.

Red Mist strapped a small pack to her waist and adjusted the weapons on her back. "The usual," she said with a shrug, her tone almost casual. "Spirits, beasts, the terrain itself. It's treacherous, but manageable if you're prepared."

Wakamono's fingers instinctively brushed the hilt of his katana, the familiar weight comforting him. He nodded, determination setting in. "I'm ready."

Red Mist gave him a brief nod of approval. "Good. You'll need to be. The mountain path is no place for carelessness. Stay sharp, stay close, and listen to everything I say."

Wakamono stood a little taller, feeling the seriousness of the mission settle on his shoulders. "I understand."

Red Mist's gaze softened, but only for a brief moment. She was a mentor, but in moments like these, Wakamono could sense the protective instinct she carried for him. "Wakamono, this mission is different. Shiro isn't just another spirit or beast we have to face. Whatever he's become, he used to be a Kōken—a powerful one. That means we have to be cautious, and you need to be on guard at all times."

Wakamono took a deep breath, feeling the weight of her words. Shiro wasn't just some ordinary threat. He had been one of them, a Kōken, trained and skilled. If he had truly turned from the path, that made him dangerous in ways Wakamono wasn't sure he fully understood yet.

"I'll be ready," Wakamono said, his voice steady.

Red Mist offered a slight nod, satisfied with his response. She turned back to her pack and began placing the last few items inside, her movements once again becoming mechanical, efficient.

"We'll leave before dawn," she said over her shoulder. "I have to go out, but I'll be back soon. Get some rest. We'll need every ounce of strength on that mountain."

Wakamono nodded, watching as she finished her preparations. He knew what the mountain paths could be like—he'd heard stories from traveling merchants in the past. Narrow ridges, sudden rockslides, steep drops, and, worst of all, the creatures that claimed the higher altitudes as their territory.

Red Mist reached for her katana, sliding it into its sheath with a practiced motion. The sound was like a whisper in the room, a subtle reminder of the dangers they would soon face. She glanced at Wakamono one last time before heading to the door.

"Be ready," she said quietly, her hand on the doorframe. "And remember—stay focused. The mountains don't forgive mistakes."

Wakamono watched her leave, his mind still buzzing with everything that had happened today. Shiro. The shortcut. The dangers ahead. There were so many unknowns, but Wakamono felt a strange excitement growing within him. Whatever awaited them in that mountain, he knew it would be another test of his abilities—and of the path he had chosen to follow.

He stepped toward his own pack and began preparing. His mind was full of questions, but he kept his focus on the task at hand. He'd need to be ready for anything.

AS RED MIST AND Wakamono climbed the narrow mountain path, the forest around them thickened, the trees growing taller and closer together, casting long shadows that blanketed the ground. The air was cool and damp, filled with the earthy scent of moss and pine. Above, the sky was obscured by the dense canopy, only faint streaks of light breaking through the leaves. The path wound its way up the mountain, rocky and treacherous, with a steep drop-off on one side. The sound of distant wind echoed in the valleys below, adding to the sense of isolation.

Wakamono walked in silence, his mind lingering on the rumors they had heard in the marketplace. Shiro—a name that now seemed to hang heavily between him and Red Mist. He had sensed something shift in her demeanor the moment they heard it. She was quieter than usual, her focus seemingly split between the dangerous path ahead and thoughts she wasn't sharing.

Finally, as they navigated a particularly narrow stretch of the trail, Wakamono broke the silence.

"What was he like?"

"Shiro..." she said, her voice low and measured, as though she were piecing together her thoughts carefully. Wakamono glanced at her, waiting for her to continue. "When we were apprentices, he was strong, determined, always pushing himself—and me—to be better. We were rivals, in a way. Constantly competing to prove ourselves."

Wakamono nodded, listening intently. This was the most she had ever spoken about her past, about the people she had trained with. He had always been curious, but she rarely opened up about her experiences before becoming a Kōken. "You said you trained together for a long time, right?" he asked.

Red Mist kept her gaze forward, her expression hard to read. "Yes, under the same master. Shiro and I were... close, in some ways. We fought alongside each other, faced death together. That kind of bond—it's hard to explain. But there was always something different about him."

Wakamono could hear the weight in her voice, the mixture of fondness and regret. "Different how?" he asked.

"He was always restless," Red Mist continued. "Even as we neared completion of our training to become Kōken, Shiro never seemed satisfied. He wanted more. He thought we should have more control, more say in how things were done. I think he saw the Kōken code as limiting—too focused on service, on others."

Wakamono frowned, trying to reconcile this version of Shiro with the one he had imagined. "Did you know he was going to leave?"

Red Mist paused, her steps slowing as she recalled the last time she had seen Shiro. "Not exactly," she said, her voice softer now. "The last time I saw him, he told me he was going to start working as a Kōken in another part of the region. He seemed... different then. More distant. But I didn't think much of it at the time. We had both finished our training, and it wasn't uncommon for Kōken to part ways after that. But now..."

Her voice trailed off, and Wakamono could sense the uncertainty in her words. She hadn't known what had happened to Shiro after he left. The rumors they had overheard in the marketplace had been as much of a shock to her as they had been to him.

"So, you didn't know?" Wakamono asked, carefully.

Red Mist shook her head. "No. Not until now." She stopped walking for a moment, turning to face Wakamono. Her gaze was sharp, but there was a flicker of something else—concern, perhaps. "Shiro was always one to push boundaries, but to hear that he's taken control of a town, demanding tribute... it's hard to imagine him departing so far from the path."

Wakamono was quiet, absorbing her words. The more he heard, the more he could sense how deeply this affected her. This wasn't just another mission to Red Mist. It was personal. But Wakamono couldn't shake the feeling that there was more to the story—something she wasn't saying.

They continued up the path, the wind picking up slightly as they gained altitude. The mountains stretched out ahead of them, a daunting and vast expanse of wilderness. Wakamono felt the weight of the journey ahead, not just in the physical distance, but in the emotional terrain they were about to cross.

"Why do you think he changed?" Wakamono asked after a long pause.

Red Mist's expression darkened. "I don't know. Maybe it was always there, beneath the surface, and I didn't see it. Or maybe... something external influenced him." She took a deep breath, her voice steady but heavy with unspoken emotions. "But that's why we need to find out. We need to see if the man I once knew is still there—or if he's truly lost."

Wakamono felt a knot form in his stomach. For the first time since he'd started training under Red Mist, he wondered if this mission might be too much for her. He had never seen her so uncertain, so haunted by the past. And the fact that she didn't know what they would find in Hanamachi only made the journey feel more perilous.

As the path narrowed again, the ground beneath their feet becoming more uneven, Wakamono glanced at Red Mist. She was focused, determined as always, but there was an edge to her that hadn't been there before.

Wakamono remained quiet, his mind racing. He tightened his grip on his katana and forced himself to push aside the doubt. Whatever awaited them in Hanamachi, they would face it together. But for the first time, he wasn't sure if even Red Mist knew what that truly meant.

The wind howled through the mountain pass as they ascended, and, in the distance, the peaks of surrounding ridges loomed dark and ominous against the sky.

後見

As Red Mist and Wakamono continued their journey through the rugged mountain path, the air grew colder and the trees grew sparser, their twisted trunks weathered by years of harsh wind. The sky overhead had darkened with thick clouds, casting the terrain below in deep, shadowy hues. A dark forest bordered the path on one side, a sheer drop on the other. Jagged rocks jutted from the cliffs, and the trail was narrow and treacherous, with loose gravel and crumbling edges that dropped steeply into the fog-covered valley far below.

Wakamono's eyes darted to every shadow, his hand instinctively gripping the hilt of his katana as they walked. The silence between him and Red Mist felt heavy, and he couldn't shake the uneasy feeling that something was watching them. The mountain air was sharp with tension, and each footstep seemed to echo ominously through the quiet expanse.

Suddenly, a deep, guttural roar echoed from the dense thicket up ahead, followed by the violent crack of splintering wood. Wakamono froze, his heart pounding as the sound reverberated through the trees. Red Mist's hand shot out, motioning for him to stay still. Her eyes scanned the darkening forest, her body tensed like a coiled spring, ready for anything.

Out of the shadows emerged the hulking figure of a hibagon—a monstrous, ape-like creature, larger than any beast Wakamono had ever seen. Its fur was a matted, filthy black, streaked with mud and debris from the mountain. Its eyes glowed a sickly yellow, filled with primal rage and hunger. Massive, muscular arms hung low at its sides, the hands tipped with sharp claws that scraped against the rocky ground. It stood nearly twice Wakamono's height, its breath steaming in the cold air, nostrils flaring as it caught their scent.

Wakamono's breath hitched in his throat as the hibagon let out another roar, louder this time, sending birds scattering from the nearby trees. The creature's massive form was terrifying, with its gnarled teeth bared and its muscles rippling with every movement. It lumbered toward them with surprising speed, its heavy steps shaking the ground beneath them.

"Stay back!" Red Mist's voice was sharp, pulling Wakamono out of his momentary shock. She drew her katana with a swift, practiced motion, her gaze never leaving the approaching monster. Wakamono followed suit, drawing his own blade, though his hands trembled ever so slightly as the hibagon charged.

The beast lunged, swinging one of its massive arms toward Red Mist with terrifying force. She sidestepped the attack, her movements quick and precise, but the force of the blow sent a nearby tree crashing to the ground. Wakamono ducked just in time to avoid the splintering branches, his heart racing as the battle erupted into chaos.

The hibagon let out another enraged roar, its breath visible in the cold mountain air. It swiped again, this time at Wakamono, its claws whistling through the air. He barely managed to dodge, feeling the rush of wind as the claws missed him by inches.

Wakamono countered with a swift strike, his blade finding its mark on the creature's side. The hibagon bellowed in pain, stumbling back but not falling. Blood—thick and dark—began to seep from the wound, but it seemed only to enrage the beast further.

Red Mist moved with deadly precision, darting in and out of the hibagon's reach, her katana slashing across its thick hide with every opportunity. But the hibagon was relentless, its powerful arms swinging wildly, smashing through trees and sending debris flying in all directions.

The creature grabbed a fallen tree trunk and hurled it toward them. Wakamono barely had time to react, diving to the ground as the massive log flew over the cliff edge behind him, sending rocks and dirt tumbling into the valley below.

Wakamono scrambled to his feet, eyes wide, as he realized how close he had come to being crushed. The cliff edge was crumbling beneath them, the narrow path becoming even more dangerous as the hibagon continued its assault.

"We need to drive it back!" Red Mist shouted over the din of the battle. She slashed at the creature's legs, hoping to force it to retreat, but the hibagon was unyielding. It charged again, roaring as its massive fists slammed into the ground, sending shockwaves through the earth. Wakamono stumbled, his balance momentarily lost, but he quickly regained his footing.

With a swift, powerful strike, Red Mist landed a deep cut across the hibagon's chest. The creature howled in pain, staggering back, blood pouring from its wounds. It was badly injured now, its movements slower, more erratic, but still filled with dangerous fury.

Wakamono saw his chance. He rushed forward, his katana gleaming in the dim light, and struck at the hibagon's side, driving the blade deep into its flesh. The creature bellowed in agony, falling to its knees, its breath ragged and uneven.

Red Mist stood back, watching as the hibagon knelt before them, beaten but not yet dead. Wakamono raised his katana for the final blow, but Red Mist's voice stopped him.

"Wait."

He turned to her, confused. "It's not finished. We can end this."

Red Mist's eyes softened as she approached the creature. "It's not our place to kill it. It was only defending its territory."

Wakamono hesitated, lowering his blade slightly as he looked down at the hibagon. Its yellow eyes were filled with pain and rage, but there was no malice, no evil intent. It was simply a creature of the mountains, fighting to survive.

Red Mist sheathed her katana and pulled out the healing blade from Wakamono's pack, its broken edge gleaming faintly in the cold air. Wakamono watched in stunned silence as she approached the hibagon, carefully brushing the blade over and into its wounds.

The blade vibrated softly, its power flowing into the creature's injured body. Slowly, the bleeding stopped, and the wounds began to close. The hibagon's breathing steadied, its pain easing as the healing took effect.

When the wounds were healed, the hibagon rose to its feet, towering over them once more. Wakamono tensed, ready to defend himself, but the hibagon did not attack. It simply stood there for a moment, watching them with its glowing eyes.

Without a sound, the hibagon turned and lumbered away, disappearing into the thick fog that clung to the mountains. Wakamono stood there, his heart still pounding, unsure of what to make of the encounter.

Red Mist sheathed the healing blade and turned to Wakamono. "Not every battle needs to end in death."

Wakamono looked down at his katana, the weight of the lesson sinking in. He had been ready to kill, to end the threat, but Red Mist had shown mercy—even to a creature as dangerous as the hibagon.

As they resumed their journey, Wakamono couldn't help but feel a strange mix of emotions. The hibagon had been a threat, and yet they had saved it. It hadn't shown any gratitude, hadn't even acknowledged their act of mercy. It simply vanished into the mountains, as wild and dangerous as ever.

The encounter weighed heavily on Wakamono's mind as they continued through the treacherous path. He glanced at Red Mist, seeing the calm resolve in her expression, but inside, he felt the gnawing question: was mercy always the right choice?

後見

As Red Mist and Wakamono began their descent from the craggy peaks of the mountain, the dense forest gradually thinned out, giving way to a breathtaking view of the valley below. The late afternoon sun bathed the scene in a golden glow, casting long shadows over the landscape. Wakamono stopped for a moment, his breath catching in his throat as he took in the view.

Hanamachi stretched out before them like a tapestry woven from fields and winding rivers. The town was nestled in the heart of the valley, surrounded by vibrant farmlands, the patchwork of crops shimmering in shades of green and gold. Neat rows of rice paddies glistened in the distance, the water reflecting the warm light of the sun. Beyond the paddies, orchards full of fruit trees stood in bloom, their blossoms painting the land with soft pinks and whites.

Smoke rose lazily from the chimneys of the town's many buildings, indicating the hearths of homes and bustling inns. Wakamono could just make out the stone walls that encircled the heart of the town, marking its more affluent district. From this distance, Hanamachi looked like a beacon of prosperity and order, its wide streets lined with tall, elegant structures built from sturdy timber and tiled roofs.

"It's beautiful," Wakamono said quietly, more to himself than to Red Mist. It was clear that Hanamachi was thriving—at least on the surface. There was something almost idyllic about the scene: the people in the fields tending to their crops, the wide, cobblestone streets lined with vendors' stalls and market squares. From this vantage, it was hard to imagine that anything was amiss.

To the north of the town, just beyond the stone walls, a sprawling estate dominated the hillside. Surrounded by meticulously manicured gardens and towering gates, the estate stood apart from the rest of Hanamachi, its grandeur unmistakable even from this distance. The elegant wooden structure, crowned with a roof of ornate tiles, gleamed in the sunlight. Though too far to discern specific details, Wakamono guessed that this must be the residence of someone important—perhaps a noble or a lord.

As they descended further, he noticed the farmlands that sprawled outward from the town, expanding like a patchwork of prosperity into the valley. The farmers worked diligently, the rows of crops immaculately maintained, as though every inch of land was used to its fullest potential. Yet, there was a stillness to their movements that Wakamono couldn't quite place—a kind of weariness that seemed at odds with the town's apparent wealth.

"They're doing well for themselves," Wakamono remarked, his eyes scanning the scene below. "It doesn't look like a place in need of Kōken."

Red Mist remained silent for a moment, her sharp gaze sweeping over the town and its outskirts. She had seen prosperous towns before—ones that looked as peaceful as this—but her years of experience had taught her that appearances were often deceiving. Her jaw tightened as her eyes lingered on the distant estate.

"We'll see," she finally said, her tone cautious. "Prosperity can hide many things, Wakamono. Don't be so quick to trust what you see on the surface."

They resumed their descent, the air growing warmer and thicker as they left the cool mountain winds behind. Wakamono couldn't help but feel a flicker of curiosity, even excitement, as they neared the town. Hanamachi looked like everything he had ever imagined—lush fields, tall buildings, and the promise of something greater. But there was a tension in the air, a subtle unease that Wakamono couldn't yet identify.

3
三

AS RED MIST AND Wakamono drew closer to Hanamachi, the air of prosperity that had dominated their
first glimpse of the town began to fade. The grandeur
of the valley view, with its gleaming estate and lush
farmlands, was quickly replaced by something grit-
tier—less polished. The fields that had seemed so
orderly from a distance revealed a different truth up
close.

Wakamono noticed that many of the outlying farms
weren't as prosperous as they appeared. The rows of
crops that once seemed to shimmer with vitality now
looked wilted and uneven, their soil cracked and dry in
places. The farmers worked with a visible heaviness,
their movements slow, weighed down by exhaustion.
Their clothes, once assumed to be the simple garments of a hard-working people, now appeared frayed
and patched, worn from years of overuse. Some of
the farmers glanced up as Red Mist and Wakamono
passed, their faces gaunt, their eyes hollow.

A group of young children stood near the edge of a field, their clothes no better than the farmers'. They played in silence, without the usual shouts of excitement that Wakamono had always associated with children. One boy, no older than eight, stared at Wakamono with a gaze far too serious for someone his age, as if he had already seen too much of the world's hardships. Wakamono's stomach tightened at the sight.

As they approached the town's outer edges, the poverty became even more stark. The outskirts were lined with cramped, dilapidated houses made from weathered wood and cracked stone. Some buildings had missing roof tiles or sagging walls, and others looked abandoned entirely, their doors hanging open, revealing empty interiors. The air here was thick with dust, the scent of neglect heavy in Wakamono's nose.

Wakamono's eyes flicked toward Red Mist, hoping to gauge her reaction, but her expression was unreadable, her face set in its usual calm, focused manner. She had no need to say anything—he could feel the tension in the air, the quiet that clung to the streets like a shroud. Even a marketplace, which they soon passed, was strangely subdued. The usual clamor of merchants hawking their wares was absent. Instead, the market stalls were sparsely filled, and the few vendors who were present showed a kind of resigned desperation. Some sold small amounts of dried fish or withered vegetables. Their smiles, when they tried to engage with passing customers, never reached their eyes.

Wakamono noticed the looks they were receiving. Some townspeople eyed them with open curiosity, others with thinly veiled suspicion. Most, however, kept their distance, their gazes filled with a fear that Wakamono could not yet understand. There was a heaviness in their stares, as though they were trapped beneath the weight of something far larger than themselves. The word "Kōken" could be heard, whispered in the crowd.

A man, hunched over and dressed in ragged clothing, scurried past them, his head lowered. As he hurried by, Wakamono caught a glimpse of something strange—a mark on the man's wrist. It was a faint red brand, shaped like a broken circle. Before Wakamono could ask Red Mist about it, the man disappeared into a narrow alleyway, his figure swallowed by the shadows.

"This isn't what I expected," Wakamono muttered, his voice low. He had imagined a town filled with bustling activity, a place where the people thrived under the protection of a powerful Kōken. Instead, Hanamachi felt like a town living in the shadow of something dark and unseen.

Red Mist glanced at him, her eyes narrowing slightly. "Appearances are often deceiving," she said quietly. "The closer we get, the more we'll see the truth."

They walked further into the town, the buildings growing taller, the streets more crowded. Wakamono noticed that the center of Hanamachi, with its polished stone roads and decorative lanterns, was a stark contrast to the outer slums they had passed. Here, the houses were larger, their windows adorned with fine silks and elegant wooden carvings. Some of the wealthier townspeople strolled leisurely through the streets, their clothes clean and well-made. But even here, there was a stiffness to their movements, as if every action was measured, every word carefully chosen.

"They're afraid," Wakamono said suddenly, realizing what it was he had been sensing all along. "Even the rich are afraid."

Red Mist nodded, her gaze fixed on a large building at the end of the street—a grand estate, with tall gates and ornate designs. "Yes. Fear is a powerful tool, Wakamono. It can build empires... but it can also destroy them."

As they approached the gates, the townspeople's whispers grew louder. Wakamono overheard fragments of conversations—mentions of Shiro's name, spoken in tones of both reverence and fear. Some people glanced at Red Mist and Wakamono with a spark of hope in their eyes, while others quickly averted their gaze, as if associating with strangers was dangerous.

Wakamono felt a knot of unease settle in his chest. He had always admired the Kōken for their strength and honor, for their ability to protect the weak. But here, in Hanamachi, things seemed... different. The people didn't just have protection—they were living under a shadow, one that felt suffocating and inescapable.

"We'll find Shiro," Red Mist said, her voice steady but edged with a tension Wakamono had rarely heard from her. "And when we do, we'll learn just how far he's fallen."

With that, they moved toward the grand gates that marked the entrance to what had to be Shiro's estate, the town of Hanamachi heavy with tension behind them. The towering iron bars cast long shadows across the cobbled street. The gate was flanked by two guards, both clad in black armor emblazoned with a symbol Wakamono didn't recognize—a demonic face with a blade behind or through it. They stood tall and imposing, their hands resting casually on the hilts of their weapons, as if they expected no real challenge today.

As Red Mist neared, the older of the two guards stepped forward, his expression cold and unyielding. His lips curled into a smirk as he gave her a slow, mocking once-over. "What business do you have here?" he asked, his tone dripping with condescension. "This area is not open to wanderers."

Wakamono's fists clenched at his sides, a surge of anger flaring in his chest. These men had no idea who Red Mist was, no idea of her rank and power. He wanted to speak, to demand entry, but a subtle glance from Red Mist stopped him. She remained calm, her gaze fixed steadily on the guard, as though she hadn't even noticed his smugness.

"We've come to speak with Shiro," Red Mist said evenly. "I'm an old acquaintance."

The younger guard, standing behind the older one, shifted uncomfortably at her words. He seemed less confident, as though the very mention of Shiro had unsettled him. His eyes darted to the older guard, waiting for his reaction.

The smirking guard chuckled, his hand waving dismissively. "Old acquaintances, eh? Well, I'm afraid Master Shiro doesn't take kindly to uninvited guests. You're not on his list. Best turn around and go back the way you came."

Wakamono took a step forward, his heart pounding with frustration. "Do you know who you're speaking to?" he snapped, his voice harder than he'd intended. "This is Red Mist, Kōken of Sanpuku City."

The older guard barely glanced at Wakamono, his smirk deepening into a full grin. "Ah, so we've got a little hero in training, do we?" He leaned forward slightly, his eyes locking with Wakamono's. "Let me give you some advice, boy. Around here, titles and names don't mean much. The only thing that matters is power, and Master Shiro is the one who has it."

Wakamono felt a rush of heat climb up his neck, his hands itching draw his katana. But before he could move, Red Mist's hand gently touched his arm. It was a light gesture, but it carried the weight of command.

"Wakamono," she said softly, her tone steady and unbothered.

Reluctantly, Wakamono stopped, biting his tongue as his anger simmered beneath the surface. How could she remain so calm in the face of such disrespect? He wanted to demand justice, to force their way through the gates and confront Shiro, but Red Mist stood as though the guard's words had no effect on her at all.

The older guard's grin widened, clearly pleased by Wakamono's restraint—or perhaps amused by what he saw as Red Mist's submission. He leaned back against the gatepost, crossing his arms over his chest.

"Smart choice," he said lazily, his tone patronizing. "Master Shiro's got no time for people like you. If you really want to talk to him, you'll need a better reason than 'old acquaintances.' So why don't you two go back to whatever hole you crawled out of?"

Wakamono's fists tightened again, but this time he didn't move. Red Mist, still composed, met the guard's gaze with her usual unwavering calm. There was no anger in her eyes, no trace of frustration—just an almost unsettling stillness.

"Thank you for your time," Red Mist said coolly, turning on her heel with a grace that left the guards blinking in confusion. "We'll be on our way."

Wakamono followed her, his frustration boiling over as they walked back down the street, away from the estate. "Why did you let him talk to you like that?" he hissed under his breath. "We could've pushed through, forced our way in—"

Red Mist cut him off with a slight shake of her head. "Force doesn't solve everything, Wakamono. Especially here. We don't know enough yet."

"But he insulted you," Wakamono muttered, feeling the sting of the guard's words on Red Mist's behalf. "They think we're weak."

"They think what Shiro wants them to think," she replied calmly, her eyes scanning the streets ahead. "Besides, they're just guards following orders. They don't know any better."

As they moved away from the guards, one could be heard saying "Too bad she didn't try a little harder. We might have had some fun, know what I mean?"

Wakamono frowned, but he couldn't argue with her logic. As much as it irked him to let the guard's arrogance go unchecked, he knew Red Mist was right. Charging into Shiro's estate without understanding the situation would have been foolish, and it would've made things worse for them in the long run.

"We'll learn what we need," Red Mist said, her voice firm but quiet. "We don't need to go through those gates to understand what's happening in Hanamachi."

Wakamono nodded, though his fists remained clenched. Red Mist was the picture of patience and self-control, qualities he knew he still had to master. But as they walked further away from Shiro's estate, Wakamono's mind kept drifting back to the smug grin on the guard's face, and the way he'd spoken so dismissively of Red Mist's title and power.

後見

The tavern was a dimly lit, smoky place, its air thick with the scent of sour ale and burnt meat. Red Mist and Wakamono pushed open the heavy wooden door, stepping into a world far removed from the busy market streets they had passed through earlier. The patrons sat huddled in groups, speaking in low voices, their faces obscured by the flickering light of oil lamps and the haze of pipe smoke. The smell of stale beer and rice wine lingered, mixing with the earthy scent of damp wood and sweat.

Wakamono glanced around, taking in the different faces that populated the room. A few men sat at a corner table, hunched over their mugs of ale, speaking in hushed tones. Their clothes were rough and torn, their faces gaunt and worn, as though the weight of the world had crushed them into the very ground they worked on. One of them, an older man with sunken cheeks, stared vacantly into his drink, muttering to himself.

"That one," the bartender spoke softly as Red Mist and Wakamono approached the bar, "used to own one of the biggest farms in the valley. Rich man, proud too. But now look at him. Lost everything."

Wakamono raised an eyebrow, glancing at the ragged man in the corner. "What happened?"

The bartender, a stocky man with graying hair and a thick beard, leaned forward, wiping his hands on a stained rag. His voice was low, as though speaking too loudly might summon trouble. "Master Shiro took his land. Said it wasn't being worked efficiently enough, meanin' his tributes were lacking, so he sold it off. Now the poor soul works as a farmhand for someone else, drinkin' his nights away."

Red Mist, standing beside Wakamono, listened with an unreadable expression, her arms crossed. "And the others?" she asked, her voice calm but probing.

The bartender gave a small, bitter chuckle. "Some are doin' well. Some ain't. Depends on which side of Shiro's favor you find yourself on. The wealthy in here, they're the ones who've kept their land, paid the tributes, kept Shiro happy. But it ain't like it used to be. Even they're starting to worry."

Wakamono glanced toward a group of wealthier patrons seated near the hearth. They were dressed in finer clothes, their laughter loud and boisterous. One man—a large, round fellow with a red face and gold rings on his fingers—was boasting about the quality of his crops, how he'd expanded his fields recently. "Shiro's protection has been a blessing, really," the man said, loudly enough for everyone to hear. "Kept the akuma and the beasts away. Worth every coin."

The bartender snorted and shook his head. "They like to forget the price we've paid."

Wakamono frowned. "akuma?" he asked, turning his attention back to the bartender. "What akuma?"

The bartender's face darkened, and he glanced around the room as if to make sure no one else was listening. He leaned in closer, his voice dropping to a near whisper. "This was a long time ago, before Shiro came to power. Hanamachi was...well, prosperous, but vulnerable. A big target, bein' tucked away in the valley like this, isolated-like. There wasn't no protection back then, not until Shiro arrived."

He paused, his eyes narrowing as he recalled the memory. "The akuma came out of nowhere, one day. Black as night, eyes like glowing embers. It was a nightmare made flesh. It didn't care about crops or coins—it cared about chaos, death. Ripped through the farms, set buildings ablaze, killed anyone who stood in its path. We were helpless, most of us too scared to even fight back, not that we could have. For weeks, the town suffered."

Wakamono's breath hitched as he listened to the tale, imagining the terror that must have gripped the people of Hanamachi. He'd read about akuma before—demons, spirits of malevolence born from darkness, bent on destruction. "What happened next?"

"Shiro," the bartender replied, with a heavy sigh. "He showed up out of nowhere. A wandering Kōken, just passing through, or so we thought. But when he saw what was happening, he didn't hesitate. He went straight to the akuma, blade in hand. The fight...well, it was something to see. No one thought a man could stand against a demon like that. But Shiro, he didn't just stand. He won. Drove the akuma out of the valley, and saved Hanamachi."

The bartender's eyes glimmered for a moment, a trace of the old admiration still lingering in his voice. But then his face hardened again. "After that, everyone worshipped him. Threw gifts at his feet, begged him to stay. Said he'd keep us safe. At first, he was a hero. But over time...well, power changes people, doesn't it?"

Red Mist remained silent, her expression impassive as the bartender spoke. Wakamono, however, could feel the weight of the man's words pressing down on him. Shiro had once been a savior, a protector. But something had shifted, something had twisted in him. Wakamono glanced at Red Mist, wondering what she was thinking, but her face gave nothing away.

Before they could ask anything further, the door to the tavern burst open, and a young guard rushed in, the same one from the gate, his face pale and nervous. He spotted Red Mist and Wakamono immediately and hurried over to them, bowing his head in apology.

"Forgive me," he said, breathless, clearly anxious. "Master Shiro was unaware of your presence. He wishes to see you both at once."

Red Mist arched an eyebrow but said nothing, merely exchanging a glance with Wakamono. The tension in the air was palpable as the guard stood, awaiting their response.

Wakamono could feel his pulse quicken. This was it—their chance to finally face Shiro. To see the man who had once fought alongside Red Mist and understand what had led him down this path.

Red Mist gave a short nod. "Lead the way."

The guard bowed again, then quickly turned on his heel, beckoning them to follow. As they left the tavern, Wakamono couldn't shake the unease that had settled in his chest. The town's past was a story of heroism, but its present...something was deeply wrong here, and whatever they were about to face, it wasn't going to be easy.

SHIRO'S ESTATE STOOD LIKE a monument to power, sprawling across the landscape at the far end of the town. Wakamono had never seen anything like it. Unlike the humble villages he grew up in and the simple quarters he shared with Red Mist, Shiro's estate was an embodiment of excess and authority. Tall stone walls surrounded the compound, with ornate iron gates swung open to allow them entry. The winding path to the main house was lined with lanterns, each flickering softly as dusk settled in, casting long shadows across the meticulously kept gardens.

Wakamono's eyes roved over the estate as they approached, noting the lush greenery and intricate carvings that adorned the walls of the main building. The building itself loomed over them, its roof curved like the temples of the mountain shrines, but its structure modern, with massive beams and decorated with expensive looking woods and lacquered surfaces. The sheer scale of it all made him feel small, insignificant—a boy far from his farm, standing in the shadow of a man who had mastered not just the blade, but the art of dominance.

"Master Shiro sure knows how to live," Wakamono muttered under his breath, glancing at Red Mist to gauge her reaction. But as always, her face was unreadable, her calm demeanor betraying none of the thoughts running through her mind.

A servant greeted them at the grand doors, bowing respectfully before ushering them inside. The opulence continued indoors—walls lined with scrolls of exquisite art, hallways adorned with rare and valuable tapestries. The floors beneath their feet were polished to a mirror-like shine, reflecting the dim lanterns that illuminated the vast entry hall. It was clear that Shiro had risen far beyond the humble life of a Kōken.

Wakamono couldn't help but be impressed. This wasn't the life of a rogue or a fallen warrior. This was a man who had carved out his place in the world, someone who had built something grand from the ashes of a ruined town. Yet, despite the awe he felt, there was an unease gnawing at him—a lingering doubt that something darker lay beneath the surface.

The servant led them through the house and out into a garden courtyard, where Shiro stood, waiting. He was dressed simply, in stark contrast to the extravagance around him, his robes loose and practical, yet still refined. His long black hair was tied back, his face clean-shaven, but his eyes...there was something unsettling in them. They gleamed with a sharpness that spoke of ambition, hunger.

When Shiro's gaze fell upon Red Mist, his smile broadened, but it was the kind of smile that didn't show in his eyes. "Red Mist," he greeted her, his voice smooth and measured, "It has been too long."

"Shiro," Red Mist replied, her tone colder than Wakamono had ever heard it. She didn't return the smile. She kept her distance, her hand resting on the hilt of her katana.

Shiro chuckled softly, shaking his head. "Still the same, I see. Always on edge, always ready to draw your weapon."

Wakamono stood slightly behind Red Mist, his gaze shifting between the two of them. He hadn't known much about their history, but now, standing in the middle of this grand estate, he could feel the tension between them—years of shared experiences, memories, and something else. Something heavier, darker.

"I'm here for answers, Shiro," Red Mist said, her voice firm, though calm. "What have you done to this town? You were a protector, once. A Kōken. Now I hear whispers of tyranny and oppression. This—" She motioned to the estate. "—this is not what we were trained to do."

Shiro's smile faltered slightly, but only for a moment. He gestured to the gardens around them, the estate beyond. "And yet, look at what I've built. Hanamachi was once a town teetering on the edge of destruction. When I arrived, it was on the brink of collapse—ravaged by akuma, overrun by chaos. I brought order. I brought peace."

"At what cost?" Red Mist shot back. "You took their land, their freedom. You're no better than the monsters we fight."

Shiro's gaze hardened, but he kept his voice controlled. "The world isn't like the ideals we once held, Red Mist. It's harsh, and sometimes it requires harsh methods. Control is necessary. Power is necessary. Without it, this town would fall again. I've given them protection. Stability. They owe me their loyalty."

Red Mist took a step forward, her hand tightening around the hilt of her blade. "That's not the oath we took as Kōken. We protect the people, not rule them. We are their shields, not their masters."

Shiro's smile returned, though now it was colder, more sinister. "Naïve as ever, I see. The world isn't that simple anymore. You think that by swinging a blade a few beasts, you can solve everything? That's not enough. Power is what keeps people in line, what keeps them safe. You can't protect without oversight. You can't lead without making sacrifices."

Wakamono watched the exchange, his heart pounding in his chest. The words Shiro spoke resonated with a part of him—a part that had always questioned the simplicity of the Kōken path. Red

Mist's way was noble, yes, but was it practical? Was it enough?

But seeing the pain in Red Mist's eyes, the determination in her stance, Wakamono knew that this wasn't just a debate. This was personal.

"You've betrayed the Kōken," Red Mist said quietly. "You've betrayed everything we stand for."

Shiro's eyes flashed with irritation. "Betrayed? No. I've adapted. I've evolved. The Kōken are relics, stuck in their ways. If you can't see that, Red Mist, then you will be left behind."

For a long moment, they stood there, the tension thick enough to cut with a blade. Wakamono felt like an outsider in the middle of a storm—caught between the ideals of his master and the cold pragmatism of Shiro. He could feel the pull of both sides, the doubt creeping into his mind.

But then Shiro's tone shifted, his voice softening as he turned to Wakamono, ignoring Red Mist's fury. "Why don't you stay here, both of you? You'll see, Red Mist—this place isn't what you think it is. You'll see what I've built, and perhaps, you'll come to understand."

Red Mist's jaw clenched, but she remained silent. Wakamono glanced at her, unsure of what to say, but in the end, it was Red Mist who gave a slow nod. "We'll stay. But don't think for a second that we've come to join you, Shiro."

Keep your friends close....

Shiro's smile widened again, but his eyes were still sharp. "Of course not. Consider it...a visit. Let me show you what I've achieved."

Wakamono didn't know what to feel. He couldn't deny the allure of what Shiro had created—the power, the control, the stability. But standing next to Red Mist, he also couldn't shake the feeling that something was terribly wrong.

後見

Wakamono sat on the edge of his bed, his eyes scanning the ornate walls of his new quarters. Everything about Shiro's estate screamed wealth, power, and excess—so different from what he had known with Red Mist. He felt restless, the events of the day swirling in his mind. The meeting with Shiro had left an uneasy feeling in his gut, one he couldn't shake.

A soft knock came at the door. Before Wakamono could respond, Red Mist entered. There was a heaviness in her expression, a shadow that darkened her usually calm demeanor. She closed the door quietly and stood for a moment, as if unsure of what to say.

Wakamono sensed the weight of what was coming. He had never seen Red Mist so visibly disturbed. "Something's bothering you," he said cautiously.

She nodded, then moved to sit across from him, her back to the window where the moonlight filtered through the shutters. The dim light cast her face in half-shadow, and her usual confidence seemed fractured.

"You've noticed how different Shiro is, from what a Kōken should be," Red Mist began, her voice low but steady.

Wakamono nodded slowly. "I have. But… he couldn't have always been like this. You two were close once, right?"

Red Mist looked away, as if the question touched on something too painful to face head-on. She let out a breath and rested her hands on her knees, fingers tightening and relaxing as memories flooded back. "We were. More than just comrades. We trained together for years, fought side by side. But there's something, Wakamono. Something I've tried to forget."

Wakamono leaned forward slightly, his curiosity piqued.

Red Mist's gaze drifted to the floor, her voice dropping even lower. "It was a mission—years ago, before Shiro and I parted ways. We were sent to deal with an oni terrorizing a village deep in the forest. It wasn't just a mindless beast. This oni was smart, calculating. It hadn't killed anyone yet, but it had them living in fear, destroying their homes, crops, livestock—everything that kept the village alive. The people were desperate."

She paused, her brow furrowing as the memories clawed their way to the surface. "Our mission was simple: subdue the oni, protect the village. But Shiro... he had other ideas. He saw it as an opportunity to prove himself, to show how powerful he was. He had always been ambitious, but back then, I thought he could still be reasoned with."

Wakamono listened intently, the tension in the room growing with every word.

"We tracked the oni into the forest, just outside the village," Red Mist continued, her voice tightening with the memory. "When we found it, it was hiding among the trees, waiting for the right moment to strike. I wanted to wait, to lure it away from the village where we could fight without endangering anyone. But Shiro... Shiro was impatient. He charged in, eager for glory."

Her eyes darkened, and she clenched her fists. "He didn't care about the villagers. He wanted to fight the oni right there, where everyone could see his 'victory.' I tried to stop him, but he wouldn't listen. He backed the oni into the village, and everything went to hell."

Wakamono's heart raced as he imagined the scene. "What happened?"

"The oni panicked," Red Mist replied, her voice now tinged with bitterness. "It rampaged through the village, tearing apart homes, smashing carts, crushing people underfoot. It was chaos—people screaming, running for their lives. The air was thick with smoke and the stench of fear. I begged Shiro to pull back, to find another way, but he was blind to it all. He only saw the oni as a prize to be claimed, a symbol of his strength."

She paused, her jaw tightening. "I fought alongside him, trying to protect the villagers as best I could, but the damage was already done. People were dying, their homes reduced to rubble. And Shiro... he reveled in it. He didn't see the destruction he caused. He only saw the moment when he drove his sword into the oni's heart, killing it in front of everyone."

Wakamono felt a knot form in his stomach. "Did the villagers...?"

"They were terrified of him," Red Mist said, her voice breaking slightly. "Some saw him as a savior, but others... they knew what he had cost them. Their homes, their loved ones, all lost because of his reck-lessness. When the oni fell, there was no celebration. Just silence. Shiro stood over the corpse, proud of his victory, while the village lay in ruins around him."

Wakamono stared at her, his throat dry. "What did he have to say afterward?"

"He justified it, of course," she spat, her bitterness sharp as a blade. "Said the oni had to be killed no matter what. That sacrifices were necessary for the greater good. But I saw it in his eyes—he didn't care about the greater good. He cared about power. About his display of superiority. And that's when I knew..."

Red Mist's voice trailed off, and she looked at Wakamono with a deep, painful sadness. "That was the last time I saw him before he left our master. I hoped... I hoped he would change. I hoped that time away from the battlefield would bring him back to the ideals we once shared. But I was clearly wrong."

There was a long, heavy silence between them, the weight of her story pressing down on both of them.

"I don't understand," Wakamono said quietly. "How could he just ignore all the suffering? How could he live with himself after that?"

Red Mist closed her eyes, her voice softening. "Some people are consumed by ambition, Wakamono. They start with good intentions, but over time, the need for power, for authority, overtakes everything else. Shiro wasn't always like this. But the path he's chosen... it's dangerous. And I fear he's only grown worse since then."

Wakamono sat in silence, the image of Shiro's cold, calculating smile fresh in his mind. For the first time, he felt the weight of doubt pressing on his chest. Could Shiro really be that far gone? And if he was, what did that mean for Wakamono's own path?

Red Mist stood slowly, her face still heavy with sorrow. "Remember this, Wakamono. The path of a

Kōken is not about glory or power. It's about service. About protecting those who can't protect themselves. Don't let Shiro's way tempt you."

"I won't," Wakamono said, though his heart was conflicted.

"And don't get comfortable. If Shiro is truly lost, we won't be here for long."

As Red Mist left his room, the memory of her story lingered like a shadow in the back of Wakamono's mind. He couldn't help but wonder if, deep down, a part of him was drawn to the power Shiro now wielded.

And as he lay down to sleep, the doubt gnawed at him, refusing to let go.

AS THEY ENTERED THE opulent training facility within Shiro's grand estate, Wakamono's gaze swept across the room, taking in the vast array of gleaming weapons, the polished stone floors, and the towering shelves filled with scrolls and training equipment. It was a sight unlike anything he had ever seen. There was a sense of power in the air, a feeling that this was a place where one could truly become something formidable.

Shiro, noticing Wakamono's awe, smiled. "Impressive, isn't it?" he said, his voice filled with a subtle pride. "This is where I've trained for years, where I honed my skills after leaving our master. A Kōken must always push themselves to the limit, always strive for more."

Wakamono nodded silently, still marveling at the sheer size and grandeur of the facility. It was nothing like the simple courtyard he was used to training in with Red Mist. Here, everything seemed elevated, refined, and luxurious—a reflection of Shiro's status and power.

Shiro stopped in the center of the room and turned to face Wakamono, a glint in his eye. "I'd like to see what Red Mist has taught you," he said, the words more of a command than a request. "Show me what you've learned. Let's see what kind of Kōken you're becoming."

Wakamono hesitated for a moment. Shiro's presence was intimidating, and the vastness of the training hall only added to his nervousness. But the part of him that longed for recognition, that wanted to prove himself, rose to the surface.

With a determined nod, he stepped forward and drew his katana. The blade gleamed under the soft light, and he could feel the weight of Shiro's eyes on him. He took a deep breath and began moving through the forms Red Mist had drilled into him over the past months. His movements were sharp and precise, the blade cutting through the air with ease.

At first, he felt confident. The familiar rhythm of the forms grounded him, and he focused on each movement, ensuring every strike, every block was executed perfectly. But as he moved deeper into the routine, Wakamono became acutely aware of Shiro's watchful gaze, and a seed of doubt began to creep in. Was this enough? Would Shiro be impressed, or was this just a pale imitation of what he expected?

When Wakamono finally finished the sequence, he turned to Shiro, breathless but hopeful. The older Kōken was silent for a moment, his expression unreadable. Then, with a slow, deliberate nod, Shiro spoke.

"Not bad," he said, though there was no real praise in his voice. "Your movements are sharp, and you've clearly been practicing. But..."

Wakamono's heart sank as the word hung in the air.

"There's more to being a Kōken than just following the forms," Shiro continued, stepping closer to Wakamono. "You've learned the basics, but you lack... creativity. You're holding back. Red Mist has taught you how to fight within the confines of tradition, but there's a whole world of possibilities out there."

Wakamono blinked, unsure how to respond. "I—"

"Let me show you," Shiro said, cutting him off. He took a step back, drawing his own katana in one fluid motion. His stance was relaxed, almost casual, but there was an undeniable power in the way he held the blade. "Come at me. Let's see how you handle a real opponent."

Wakamono swallowed hard, feeling the weight of the challenge. He had sparred with Red Mist countless times, but this felt different. Shiro was not just testing his skills—he was testing his very understanding of what it meant to be a Kōken.

With a deep breath, Wakamono tightened his grip on his katana and charged at Shiro, swinging the blade in a precise arc. Shiro deflected the attack with ease, his movements swift and efficient. Wakamono pressed on, trying to find an opening, but every strike was met with a calm, almost effortless block or dodge.

Shiro moved like water, flowing around Wakamono's attacks with a grace that bordered on arrogance. And then, just as Wakamono thought he had found an opening, Shiro's katana darted out, disarming him with a quick, sharp motion that sent Wakamono's blade clattering to the floor.

Wakamono stumbled back, shocked by the speed and precision of the move. But before he could react, Shiro stepped forward, pressing the tip of his blade against Wakamono's chest.

"You see?" Shiro said, his voice low and steady. "Red Mist has taught you how to follow the rules, how to fight with honor. But in a real fight, in the world we live in now, honor will only get you so far."

Wakamono stared at him, his chest rising and falling with heavy breaths. He didn't know what to say. He had never felt so vulnerable, so exposed.

Shiro lowered his blade and stepped back, his expression softening. "You have potential, Wakamono. I see it. But if you truly want to become strong, if you want to protect the people you care about, you need to learn to think outside the box. There are no rules in a real fight—only survival. I can show you."

Wakamono retrieved his katana from the ground, his mind racing. Shiro's words lingered in his ears, and for the first time, he wondered if Red Mist's way was enough. Was there more to being a Kōken than what he had been taught?

Shiro watched him closely, as if sensing the turmoil within Wakamono. "Think about it," he said quietly. "There's no rush. But the world is changing, and if you don't adapt... you'll be left behind."

Wakamono nodded slowly, the weight of Shiro's words pressing down on him as he sheathed his katana. He glanced toward the door, half-expecting to see Red Mist standing there, her steady presence a reminder of everything he had learned. But the room was empty, save for the two of them.

"I'll be in the courtyard," Shiro said, turning to leave. "Join me when you're ready."

Wakamono stood there for a long moment, staring at the training facility around him, the opulence and grandeur a stark contrast to everything he had known. And for the first time, doubt began to creep into his heart.

後見

Red Mist sat cross-legged in her quarters, her breath slow and steady as she entered a state of deep meditation. The room was dimly lit, a single flickering candle casting long shadows across the walls. The weight of her conversation with Wakamono still lingered in her mind, but she pushed it aside, focusing instead on the quiet hum of her breathing. Meditation was her refuge, the place where she could find clarity amidst the chaos, where she could center herself.

But today, something felt different.

The air around her seemed to thicken, growing heavy and oppressive. A chill crept up her spine, and the familiar warmth of the candlelight dimmed, leaving her in a cold, dark void. Red Mist's brow furrowed slightly, sensing an external force. She had never felt such a presence during her meditation, and though she didn't know what it was, it was undeniably malevolent.

The darkness deepened, and suddenly, she was no longer in the safety of her room. Instead, she found herself standing on a ridge overlooking the mountain city of Sanpuku. But this was not the city as she knew it—this city was different, shrouded in a thick, oppressive fog. The streets below were filled with chaos. People ran in every direction, their faces twisted in terror. The once-bustling market stalls were over-turned, their wares scattered across the cobblestones. Flames leapt from building to building, consuming the town in a furious blaze.

And there, above the burning city, flew a black banner. The crimson image of a broken katana stood out against the dark fabric, rippling ominously in the wind. Red Mist's heart sank at the sight. It was a symbol she had never seen before, yet it filled her with a deep sense of dread.

Her gaze shifted downward, toward the heart of the city, where a figure stood tall amidst the destruction. It was Wakamono, his silhouette sharp and commanding. He wore ornate armor, gleaming in the firelight, and in his hand, he held a katana. He was surrounded by men who bowed in reverence, their loyalty to him unquestionable.

A surge of power radiated from Wakamono, but it was a twisted power, dark and tainted. Red Mist tried to call out to him, to warn him, but no sound escaped her lips. Her voice was lost in the roar of the flames, drowned by the cries of the panicked towns-people. She watched in horror as Wakamono raised his katana, his expression cold and devoid of the kind-ness she had come to know.

Suddenly, the scene shifted, and Red Mist found herself standing before him. The ground beneath her feet trembled, and the once-solid earth began to crack, splitting open as if the mountain itself were tearing apart. Wakamono's gaze met hers, and she saw no recognition in his eyes—only a ruthless determination. Without hesitation, he raised his katana and struck.

She tried to block the attack, but the force behind his blow was overwhelming. Her sword fell from her grasp, clattering to the ground as Wakamono's blade pierced her chest. Pain surged through her, and she staggered back, gasping for breath. The burning city blurred around her, and she felt the heat of the flames licking at her skin.

As she fell to her knees, the image of the black banner waving triumphantly over the city filled her vision. The broken katana gleamed crimson as if it were wet, dripping with blood, and the darkness closed in around her.

The last thing she saw was Wakamono's face, unrecognizable, a cold ruler of chaos.

Then, everything went black.

Red Mist awoke with a start, her breath coming in ragged gasps. She was back in her quarters, the candle still flickering faintly beside her. Sweat beaded on her forehead, and her heart pounded in her chest, the vivid images of the vision lingering in her mind.

She sat in silence for a moment, trying to make sense of what she had seen. The horror of it all—the burning city, the people's suffering, Wakamono's rise to power—it was too much to bear. She had never doubted Wakamono's potential, but the vision... the vision showed a future she feared with all her heart.

And the presence she had felt, the dark force that had shown her this nightmare—it was unlike anything she had encountered before. She knew now that this was no ordinary vision. Something—someone—was manipulating her, guiding her to see this terrible future.

With newfound urgency, Red Mist stood and quickly made her way out of her quarters. She had to find Wakamono, to see for herself that he was still the boy she had trained, the apprentice she believed in. She had to warn him—warn him before it was too late.

But as she approached the doors to the courtyard, her steps faltered. The sounds of clashing steel echoed from the other side, and she hesitated for a moment, her mind racing. Was this the beginning of what she had seen? Had the vision already begun to take root?

Gathering her resolve, Red Mist pushed open the doors.

後見

The courtyard was a storm of motion and sound. Wakamono's breathing was labored as he circled Shiro, his katana in hand, eyes narrowed in focus. Shiro moved with the precision of a predator, his sword cutting through the air with brutal efficiency. Wakamono was drenched in sweat, his arms aching from the constant clash of blades, but he pressed on, refusing to yield.

Shiro's training was unlike anything Wakamono had experienced under Red Mist's guidance. There were no calm instructions, no moments of pause to reflect on the lessons being taught. Shiro's methods were relentless, his strikes intended not just to challenge Wakamono's skill, but to push him to his limits—to force him to act on instinct, not thought.

"You're holding back, boy," Shiro growled as his blade slammed into Wakamono's. "You think hesitation will save you? That restraint will protect you in the heat of battle?"

Wakamono gritted his teeth, parrying a particularly vicious strike. His muscles screamed in protest, but there was something about Shiro's approach that was... freeing. Under Red Mist's watchful eye, every movement had to be precise, deliberate. But here, in this whirlwind of intensity, he felt himself letting go of the rigid control he had always maintained.

Shiro's strikes were fast, heavy, each one designed to provoke a reaction. Wakamono found himself countering with more aggression, his movements less measured and more feral. He could feel the burn in his chest, the fire that Shiro was stoking with every blow. It was exhilarating.

"Good," Shiro muttered as their blades locked. He leaned in closer, his eyes gleaming with approval. "I can see it in your eyes now. The fire. You're beginning to understand what it means to fight—to truly fight."

With a grunt, Wakamono pushed back, spinning away and slashing at Shiro's exposed side. Shiro deflected the strike with ease, but a faint smile curled on his lips. He was testing Wakamono, baiting him, and Wakamono could feel the thrill of the challenge.

Wakamono lunged forward again, his katana cutting through the air in a wide arc. Shiro sidestepped, bringing his own blade down in a brutal strike that Wakamono barely managed to block. The force of the blow sent vibrations up his arms, and for a brief moment, he stumbled back, off balance.

Shiro didn't let up. He was on Wakamono in an instant, his sword flashing in a series of quick, controlled strikes. Wakamono's defenses wavered, and for a moment, he thought he might fall. But then something clicked inside him—a release of all the tension he had carried from Red Mist's teachings. He didn't need to be careful here. He didn't need to hold back.

A surge of adrenaline shot through him, and Wakamono launched forward, his katana moving with newfound freedom. He parried Shiro's strikes, countering with a speed and aggression that surprised even himself. Each swing of his blade felt lighter, more natural. The rules that Red Mist had ingrained in him—the careful, disciplined approach to combat—faded from his mind, replaced by a raw, instinctual ferocity.

Shiro stepped back, watching Wakamono with a calculating gaze. "That's it," he said, his voice almost a whisper. "Let go. Trust your instincts. No rules, only survival."

Wakamono's heart pounded in his chest, but it wasn't from fear or exhaustion. It was excitement. This—this was what Shiro had been trying to teach him. The absence of rules, the freedom to fight without constraint, without hesitation—it was liberating.

He attacked again, this time with everything he had. His blade sang through the air, striking with purpose and force. Shiro blocked each strike, but Wakamono could see the approval in his eyes. There was no need for words now—their swords spoke for them.

The clash of steel echoed through the courtyard, each strike reverberating in the crisp mountain air. The world around them faded away, leaving only the rhythm of their combat, the dance of blades.

But as Wakamono swung his katana in a wide arc, preparing to press the advantage, something caught his attention. From the corner of his eye, he saw a figure standing at the edge of the courtyard, watching them.

Red Mist.

She stood motionless, her face unreadable, but Wakamono could feel the weight of her gaze on him. For a moment, the fire inside him flickered. The exhilaration of Shiro's training was still fresh in his veins, but seeing Red Mist there—calm, composed—brought back the familiar restraint he had been trained to uphold.

Shiro noticed the change immediately. His movements slowed, and he stepped back, lowering his katana. "You're distracted," he said, his tone sharp. "Focus."

But Wakamono couldn't. The contrast between Shiro's brutal training and Red Mist's disciplined guidance weighed heavily on him. He looked at her, searching for any sign of disapproval, but her expression remained stoic.

Shiro, sensing the tension, sheathed his sword. "We'll continue this later," he said, turning his gaze toward Red Mist. "It seems we have company."

Wakamono took a step back, lowering his blade and wiping the sweat from his brow. His heart still raced, but the excitement he had felt moments ago had given way to uncertainty. The liberating freedom of Shiro's training was intoxicating, but now, with Red Mist watching, he wasn't sure what to think.

As Shiro turned to face Red Mist, a sly smile played on his lips. "Care to join us?" he asked, his voice laced with amusement. "Or are you here to lecture your apprentice on the virtues of restraint?"

Red Mist remained silent for a moment, her eyes locked on Wakamono. When she finally spoke, her voice was calm, measured. "I think you've trained enough for today."

Wakamono looked between the two of them, feeling the weight of their unspoken disagreement. The tension in the air was palpable, and as the sun began to dip lower in the sky, casting long shadows across the courtyard, he knew that this was only the beginning.

The clash between Shiro's teachings and Red Mist's values was far from over.

後見

Red Mist stood in the doorway of Wakamono's quarters, her silhouette framed by the dim light from the corridor outside. Wakamono sat on the edge of his bed, his hands still trembling from the adrenaline of the training session with Shiro. The room was small and sparse, a stark contrast to the opulence of Shiro's estate. Wakamono's katana rested against the wall, its polished blade catching the faint flicker of the lantern.

Without a word, Red Mist stepped inside, closing the door softly behind her. She moved with a grace that belied the weight of the conversation she was about to have. Wakamono glanced up at her, sensing the tension in her posture, the slight furrow of her brow. He had expected her to come—he had seen the look in her eyes as she watched him train with Shiro.

Red Mist crossed the room in silence, standing a few paces away from him. Her eyes lingered on the katana by the wall before shifting to Wakamono himself. "You're letting go," she said quietly, her voice steady but edged with concern.

Wakamono frowned, confusion crossing his face. "Letting go of what?"

"Self-control," Red Mist replied, her gaze never wavering. "Restraint. Discipline. Everything that I've taught you."

He stiffened, defensive. "Shiro's training is different, yes, but it's not wrong. Isn't it important to know how to fight without holding back? To survive?"

Red Mist sighed, moving to sit across from him. "Survival, yes. But you are not just learning to survive, Wakamono. You are learning to protect, to serve a greater purpose than just yourself. That requires more than raw power. It requires control of one's self."

Wakamono's jaw tightened. "Shiro says there are no rules in battle, only what it takes to win."

Red Mist nodded slowly, as if she had expected this. "And in that, he is right. But there's a cost. Power without restraint leads to chaos. Violence without purpose leads to destruction. I know you felt it yourself today."

Wakamono's thoughts flashed back to the training yard, to the moment when he had felt the exhilarating freedom of fighting without the rigid constraints he was used to. It had been liberating, intoxicating even, but now, in the stillness of the night, the thrill seemed hollow. He thought of the ferocity in Shiro's eyes, the relentless push for aggression, and the gnawing doubt settled in his gut.

"Shiro... he's different from what I expected," Wakamono admitted, his voice quieter now. "But maybe he's right. Maybe I need to be more like him."

Red Mist shook her head. "Shiro has forgotten the way of the Kōken. He's not fighting for others anymore. He's fighting for himself—for his power, for dominion over this town. And look where it has led him. The people fear him more than they fear the spirits and beasts. Is that what you want, Wakamono? To be feared?"

Wakamono didn't answer immediately. The image of Shiro's estate flashed in his mind—the grandeur, the respect, the power. It was tempting, so much more than the humble life he had known with Red Mist, or the small, quiet existence he had lived on the farm.

"I don't know," he finally whispered. "It's just... I've never felt that kind of strength before. When I let go, when I stopped thinking about every little move... it was like I was free."

Red Mist leaned forward, her gaze piercing. "Strength isn't just in your sword, Wakamono. It's in your heart, in your mind. Strength is knowing when to hold back, when to show mercy. That's what separates us from the ones we fight."

Wakamono looked down at his hands, the memories of their fights together—the hibagon, the kyonshii, the battles they had faced side by side—filling his mind. Red Mist had always been calm, always a master of herself. Even when they were outnumbered, even when they faced impossible odds, she never lost sight of who they were and what they stood for.

"Shiro will offer you the world, Wakamono," Red Mist said softly. "But it's a world built on fear and domination. I want you to think about what kind of person you want to be."

Wakamono's eyes flickered with uncertainty. He had looked up to Red Mist for so long, followed her teachings without question. But now, seeing Shiro's strength, his influence, Wakamono couldn't help but feel pulled in both directions.

"I will," he murmured, though even as he said it, the doubts lingered.

Red Mist stood, her presence in the room still commanding despite her calm demeanor. "I hope you do," she said, her voice soft but firm. "Because the path you choose now will shape the rest of your journey."

With that, she turned and left the room, leaving Wakamono alone with his thoughts, the weight of her words pressing down on him. The silence in the room was almost suffocating, and for the first time since he had begun his training, Wakamono wasn't sure which path he was supposed to follow.

As he lay back on his bed, staring at the ceiling, the flickering shadows from the lantern danced across the walls, and in the back of his mind, the image of Shiro's grand estate loomed like a distant temptation.

6 六

THE STREETS OF HANAMACHI were unlike anything Wakamono had ever seen. As they walked beside Shiro through the more affluent part of town, he marveled at the grandeur around him. Buildings rose higher here, their facades adorned with polished wood and intricate carvings, their roofs a brilliant array of red and gold tiles. Lanterns hung from the eaves, casting a soft, warm glow across the cobblestone streets, where merchants displayed exotic goods and finely dressed townsfolk strolled by without a care in the world. The air smelled of incense, spices, and roasted meats, wafting from the stalls that lined the streets, selling everything from rare fabrics to finely crafted weapons.

Wakamono found it hard to believe this was the same town they had approached the day before. Here, there was no sign of fear or oppression—just wealth and prosperity.

"You see, Wakamono," Shiro said as they walked, his voice smooth and confident, "this is what power can bring. Stability. Success. Safety." He gestured toward a group of well-dressed children playing with wooden toys in the street. Their laughter echoed down the alleyways.

Wakamono nodded, unable to tear his eyes away from the sights. He had never imagined such a place existed. Even Sanpuku City, with its crowded markets and vibrant life, seemed modest compared to the luxury on display here.

"These people, they have no need to fear the spirits or the beasts that haunt the lands," Shiro continued, glancing at Wakamono out of the corner of his eye. "They know that I protect them, facilitate their prosperity, and in return, they pay their tribute. It's a fair exchange, wouldn't you say?"

Wakamono hesitated, glancing over at Red Mist, who was walking silently beside them. Her expression was unreadable, her posture stiff and wary. He knew she didn't approve, but standing in the midst of such wealth, it was hard for Wakamono not to feel the pull of Shiro's words.

"You've done a lot for them," Wakamono finally replied, his voice quieter than he intended. "But... isn't there more to being a Kōken than just power and wealth?"

Shiro chuckled softly, his tone indulgent, like a teacher amused by a student's naïveté. "Of course there is. But the world is changing, Wakamono. The old ways, the ways of the Kōken... they're outdated. It's not enough to simply protect anymore. You have to guide, to command. Without leadership, the people would be lost, vulnerable to the whims of fate."

As they passed a grand courtyard, Wakamono noticed a finely dressed merchant bowing deeply to Shiro. The man's deference was immediate, and his gratitude was apparent as he offered a small chest of what appeared to be coins as a gift.

Shiro accepted it with a gracious nod but moved on quickly, not even looking back. Wakamono watched the merchant as they left, wondering if this was what power looked like—people bending at your feet, offering whatever they could in hopes of gaining favor.

"I used to think like you, Wakamono," Shiro continued, his tone growing more personal. "When I first joined the Kōken, I believed in the same ideals that Red Mist still clings to. But I learned that ideals don't protect people. Power does. Money does. I do."

Wakamono's gaze shifted to Red Mist, but she remained silent. He could see the tension in her jaw, the tightness in her grip as her hands rested on the hilt of her sword. She wasn't going to argue, not here, not now.

They moved deeper into the heart of the affluent district. The homes here were grander, their doors carved from dark mahogany, their windows adorned with fine silks that fluttered in the gentle breeze.

Wakamono noticed the people's expressions as they passed—some nodded respectfully at Shiro, others kept their heads down, too afraid to meet his gaze.

The disparity was beginning to unsettle Wakamono, but Shiro's words still rang in his ears. *Power. Wealth. Protection.*

At one point, they stopped in front of a large, open plaza, where a group of performers were putting on a play for the locals. The actors were dressed in elaborate costumes, their voices strong and confident as they told a tale of a great warrior defeating a monstrous oni. The crowd was captivated, their laughter and cheers filling the air.

"This," Shiro said, his voice low and persuasive, "is what true leadership brings. Peace. Joy. Order."

Wakamono watched the performance, his mind torn between the allure of what he was seeing and the lessons Red Mist had taught him. Was Shiro really wrong? The people here seemed happy, prosperous. Wasn't that the goal of every Kōken, to protect the people and bring peace?

But a small voice in the back of his mind reminded him of what they had seen on the outskirts of town—the fields of farmers, the broken-down homes, the worn faces of those who struggled to survive. Those people weren't here, in this part of town. They were hidden, out of sight, out of mind.

"Of course," Shiro continued, his eyes gleaming as he glanced at Wakamono, "not everyone is ready to understand the necessity of what we do. Some... cling to old ways, to old oaths. But I see something in you, Wakamono. A potential that Red Mist has only just begun to unlock."

Wakamono swallowed hard, feeling the weight of Shiro's gaze on him. He wanted to protest, to say that Red Mist's teachings had served him well, but as he looked around, at the wealth, the security, the power that surrounded them, he found himself hesitating.

Shiro's words weren't just empty promises. He had achieved something here, something tangible, something powerful.

And for the first time since he had become Red Mist's apprentice, Wakamono wasn't sure if the path of the Kōken was the only way.

Red Mist, walking beside him, remained silent, but Wakamono could feel her watching him, her presence a quiet reminder of the choice he would soon have to make.

As the din of the crowd echoed across the plaza, She finally spoke, her voice calm and measured, yet cutting through the air like a blade.

"This part of the town is certainly beautiful, Shiro, but I wonder how much these people have given up for it," she began, her eyes scanning the wealthy district with its pristine streets and opulent homes. "And not all of Hanamachi shares in this prosperity. Wakamono and I saw the other side of your city when we arrived—fields struggling to yield crops, farmers with sunken cheeks, homes barely standing." She glanced over at Shiro, her gaze sharp. "What do you have to say about them?"

Shiro didn't flinch. He turned slowly to face Red Mist, a small, almost patronizing smile playing on his lips. "The people in those parts of town," he said, "have always struggled. It is the nature of things. Not everyone can live in luxury. But they still have something they never had before: security. Thanks to me, they no longer have to fear the beasts and spirits that used to plague their lands. That is a fair trade, wouldn't you agree?"

Red Mist's brow furrowed, her expression hardening. "Security at what cost? They may not fear spirits, but they fear you. We saw a man in the tavern who lost his farm because of your... policies. You took what little they had and gave it to others, the ones who already have more than enough."

Shiro's smile faded slightly, replaced by a look of mild annoyance. "You misunderstand, Red Mist. It's not about taking from the poor and giving to the rich. It's about ensuring that those who can contribute more to the prosperity of the town are given the means to do so. It's basic economics. Those who are more capable should have more resources. It's how we all thrive."

Wakamono watched the exchange in silence, torn between the two perspectives. Shiro's words resonated with a cold logic, but Red Mist's quiet defiance stirred something deeper within him. He had seen the starving faces, the broken homes. And yet, here, in this part of town, everything seemed perfect.

"That's not the way of the Kōken," Red Mist continued, her voice steady. "We are protectors of all people, not just those who are wealthy or powerful. You've forgotten what we stand for, Shiro. Our oath was to shield the vulnerable, to fight for those who cannot fight for themselves."

Shiro's smile returned, though it was now edged with disdain. "The oath we took was made in a different time, Red Mist. The world is harsher now, more dangerous. Can't you feel the darkness coming? Ideals alone won't protect these people."

Red Mist took a slow breath, her eyes never leaving Shiro's. "You're wrong. You're not protecting them, Shiro. You're dominating them. And that's not the path of the Kōken."

Wakamono shifted uncomfortably, glancing between them. Shiro's argument was logical, efficient even. But Red Mist's words struck at his core, reminding him of the principles he had been taught. He couldn't ignore the stark contrast between the prosperity of this part of the city and the suffering they had seen in the outskirts. The very people Shiro claimed to protect, the ones who needed his protection most, were the ones barely surviving.

Shiro must have sensed Wakamono's hesitation. He placed a hand on the young apprentice's shoulder, his grip firm yet oddly comforting. "Wakamono," Shiro said, his voice soft but authoritative, "you've seen the power I've built here. You've witnessed the safety and prosperity I've created. Isn't that what being a Kōken is about? Isn't that what you want?"

Wakamono hesitated, his heart racing as he looked into Shiro's eyes. The allure of power, of control, was tempting. He could see the results—Shiro had brought stability to this town, had ended the constant threats of spirits and beasts. But at what cost?

"I..." Wakamono began, his voice faltering.

Red Mist stepped forward, her gaze softening as she looked at Wakamono. "It's easy to be blinded by power, Wakamono. But don't forget the people who live in the shadows of that power. The ones who are suffering because of it. Being a Kōken isn't about dominance. It's about balance and service."

The silence hung heavy between them, the weight of the question pressing down on Wakamono's shoulders. He glanced back at Shiro, then at Red Mist, his mind torn between the two conflicting visions of what it meant to be a Kōken.

Shiro, sensing the tension, chuckled softly. "Let's not argue over philosophy, Red Mist," he said dismissively. "You've always been too idealistic. Perhaps some time here will help you see things differently."

He gestured toward the towering buildings and the busy plaza. "Why don't you both stay for a while longer? Let Wakamono see the results of my leadership firsthand. You might find that things are not as black and white as you think."

Red Mist's jaw tightened, but she didn't protest. She knew that leaving now wouldn't solve anything. They needed more time—to learn, to understand, and to figure out what Shiro's true intentions were. To lead him back to the path. To stop him, if it came to that.

"Very well," Red Mist said quietly, though the fire in her eyes hadn't dimmed. "We'll stay."

後見

Back at Shiro's sprawling estate, Wakamono found himself standing in a grand courtyard, surrounded by ornate gardens and finely crafted stonework. The sun was beginning to dip low, casting long shadows across the grounds as Shiro led him to the center of the training space. The estate felt like a fortress of riches, far from the simple, disciplined life Wakamono had lived under Red Mist's guidance.

Shiro watched Wakamono with a calculating gaze, his arms crossed over his chest. "Show me, again, what Red Mist has taught you," he said, his voice smooth but with an edge of challenge. "Let me see how much you've grown under her tutelage."

Wakamono nodded, drawing his katana with a sharp, precise motion. The blade caught the fading light, and for a moment, the courtyard seemed quieter, as if holding its breath in anticipation. Wakamono positioned himself into a familiar stance—one of balance, focus, and control.

Shiro observed, nodding slightly as he appraised the young apprentice. "Good," he murmured. "But let's see how well you adapt to something... less predictable."

Without warning, Shiro lunged forward, unsheathing his own katana in a blur of motion. The force of his first strike sent a tremor up Wakamono's arms as he blocked it. Wakamono's eyes widened at the strength behind the blow, but he recovered quickly, shifting into the defensive forms Red Mist had drilled into him over and over.

Their blades clashed in a flurry of strikes and counters, the metallic sound echoing across the courtyard. Wakamono moved with speed and precision, just as Red Mist had taught him. His strikes were measured, his defense solid, but there was a sharpness to Shiro's movements—an irregularity that caught Wakamono off-guard more than once.

"You're holding back," Shiro said, his voice low as their blades locked. "You're still thinking like a servant, not a master. Stop focusing on form. Focus on victory."

Wakamono gritted his teeth, pushing against Shiro's strength. "Red Mist taught me to fight with self-control and honor."

Shiro scoffed, disengaging from the clash with a swift spin. "Honor is for those who can afford to lose." He struck again, his blows faster, more erratic, forcing Wakamono to react on instinct rather than form. "In real battle, there's no room for restraint."

Wakamono struggled to keep up with the barrage, his training with Red Mist suddenly feeling distant, as if the rigid structures of her lessons couldn't match the chaos Shiro was introducing. Every time Wakamono thought he had the upper hand, Shiro shifted—breaking the flow of the fight with underhanded tactics, unexpected kicks, and even a moment where he feigned weakness, only to sweep Wakamono's legs from beneath him.

Wakamono fell hard, gasping for breath as the wind was knocked out of him. Shiro stood over him, his katana hovering just inches from Wakamono's throat.

"That's the difference between your master and me," Shiro said, his tone almost fatherly, but with an edge of arrogance. "She's teaching you not to lose. I'm teaching you to win."

Wakamono's heart raced as he stared up at Shiro. His chest burned with the effort of the fight, but something deeper gnawed at him—the conflict between the honor Red Mist had instilled in him and the harsh efficiency Shiro now demonstrated.

Shiro pulled his katana back and extended a hand to Wakamono. "Get up. You're stronger than you think. But you won't unlock that strength if you keep clinging to outdated principles."

Wakamono took the offered hand, pulling himself to his feet. His body ached, but his mind was swirling. There was a cold, hard truth to Shiro's words—a truth that both fascinated and unsettled him.

Shiro sheathed his blade, a satisfied look crossing his face. "You have potential, Wakamono. I see why Red Mist took you on. But she's holding you back. She's afraid of what you could become."

Wakamono met Shiro's gaze, his hands still trembling slightly from the intensity of the sparring. "She wants me to be the best Kōken I can be."

Shiro chuckled softly, shaking his head. "No. She wants you to be like her. Limited. Controlled. That's not how the world works anymore, Wakamono." He leaned in slightly, his voice dropping to a near whisper. "There's power waiting for you. Real power. If you're willing to reach for it."

Wakamono's breath caught in his throat as he considered the implications. For a moment, he felt a flicker of something—a desire, a curiosity. The idea of having the strength to protect the people he cared about, to bring about real change, was intoxicating. But then, the image of Red Mist's calm, unwavering eyes flashed in his mind, reminding him of the discipline she had instilled in him, the lessons of balance and restraint.

"I need to think about this," Wakamono said quietly, stepping back from Shiro.

Shiro nodded, a glimmer of satisfaction in his eyes. "Of course. Take your time. But remember, the world isn't as simple as Red Mist makes it out to be. There's a reason why she lives in near-poverty while I am served every want and need by an entire town."

Wakamono turned and began walking toward the far end of the courtyard, his mind heavy with conflicting thoughts. Shiro's words had struck a chord, and for the first time, he began to wonder if there was more to being a Kōken than what Red Mist had shown him.

As he reached the edge of the courtyard, he glanced back at Shiro, who was watching him with a smile—a smile that made Wakamono feel both empowered and uneasy.

後見

Wakamono's eyes fluttered closed as exhaustion took hold, the tension of the day finally slipping away. Sleep came quickly, and with it, the dream.

He was standing atop the highest point of Sanpuku City, the wind gently tugging at his robes as they flowed around him, rich and regal. Before him stretched the entire city—prosperous, gleaming under the golden rays of the sun. The buildings were taller, more splendid than he had ever seen in waking life, their roofs adorned with intricate carvings and banners that fluttered proudly in the breeze.

But most striking of all was the banner that flew above the tallest tower. It was red with a gleaming gold symbol—a broken katana, the hilt still strong, the blade jagged yet defiant. His healing blade. He stared up at it, feeling a swell of pride in his chest. It was a symbol of his journey, of everything he had overcome. The city below thrived under that banner, protected, secure, and rich with life.

He descended the steps, and as he walked through the grand streets of the city, people bowed before him. Farmers, merchants, soldiers—all paid their respects with grateful eyes and whispers of reverence. "Lord Wakamono," they murmured. "Protector of Sanpuku."

Wakamono's heart raced with joy. He had done it. He had risen to power, and the city flourished under his careful guidance. The once-impoverished streets were filled with active markets, the air filled with laughter and song. Everything was in order—everyone was safe.

Ahead of him, two familiar figures emerged from the crowd. His father, standing tall, dressed in fine garments that were a far cry from the simple clothes of the farm. Gou's face was alight with pride as he approached Wakamono, clasping a firm hand on his shoulder.

"You've done it, son," Gou said, his voice thick with emotion. "I always knew you had it in you. The strength to protect. The power to lead."

Wakamono's chest swelled with warmth at his father's praise, the long-held tension between them dissolved in that single moment.

And beside his father stood Red Mist, her expression softened, her usual calm demeanor replaced by a rare smile. She stepped forward, her eyes shining with approval.

"I've watched you grow into the leader you were meant to be," Red Mist said, her voice steady but full of emotion. "You've surpassed even what I could have taught you."

Wakamono felt a surge of pride as he looked between them—the two most important figures in his life, standing beside him, honoring his success. This was the future he wanted—the future he deserved. The city was safe, the people happy, and those he loved most were at his side, supporting him.

Abruptly, the dream shifted, and Wakamono found himself standing at the gates of the city, his banner still flying high above the walls. His hand rested on the hilt of his katana, the blade no longer broken but whole, shimmering with power. A distant storm brewed on the horizon, but Wakamono stood tall, unafraid. He would protect the city, no matter what came.

Red Mist and his father stood with him, their faces lit with admiration.

"You are the future of the Kōken," Red Mist said quietly, her voice full of pride. "You will lead us into a new era."

Wakamono nodded, a sense of certainty filling him. This was his destiny.

But as he gazed toward the storm in the distance, the winds began to shift, growing colder. The sky darkened, the sunlight fading into an ominous gloom. The city's banners—his banners—began to whip violently in the wind, the sound harsh and unnerving. The gold of the broken katana seemed to lose its luster, the red deepening into something more sinister.

Suddenly, Wakamono's katana felt heavier in his hand, the weight pulling him down. The storm was coming closer, faster now, dark clouds swallowing the horizon and rushing toward the city with alarming speed. The once bustling streets were now eerily silent, the joyous noise replaced by a chilling, hollow echo.

He looked to Red Mist and his father, but they were gone.

Wakamono spun around, his heart pounding as the storm crashed into the city, engulfing the buildings and streets in a swirling mass of black fog. He could hear the distant cries of the people, their once-grateful voices now filled with fear and desperation.

The dream was unraveling, the idyllic vision crumbling before his eyes.

As the storm closed in, Wakamono felt something shift beneath his feet. He looked down to see the ground cracking, the stone streets splitting apart. From the cracks emerged shadows—dark, twisted shapes writhing and reaching for him.

And then, from the heart of the storm, he heard it.

A cry.

A baby's cry, piercing through the chaos, filled with sorrow and rage.

Wakamono's heart pounded as he searched the storm for the source of the cry, but all he could see was darkness.

"My baby!" a voice shrieked, loud and desperate. The voice echoed in his mind, filling him with an overwhelming sense of dread.

Suddenly, the darkness consumed him, the storm swallowing everything.

Wakamono woke with a gasp, his body drenched in sweat. His heart raced in his chest, the remnants of the dream clinging to him like a shroud. The cry still echoed in his ears, haunting him.

He sat up in bed, trying to calm his breathing, but the unsettling feeling lingered. His hands instinctively reached for his katana, the broken blade a reminder of both his past and the uncertain future that now loomed before him.

7

七

THE MORNING LIGHT FILTERED through the windows of Shiro's grand dining hall, casting a warm glow on the ornate table where Shiro and Wakamono sat. Plates of delicately arranged food lay before them, a feast of fruits, rice, and fish, far more lavish than anything Wakamono had ever experienced. Wakamono found himself eating slowly, distracted by thoughts of his dream from the night before, still unsure of its meaning.

Shiro, on the other hand, appeared entirely at ease, his demeanor casual and relaxed. He took a bite of fish, savoring the taste as though he hadn't a care in the world. "I trust you slept well?" he asked, his voice smooth as silk.

Wakamono nodded, though the dream still haunted him. "Yes... well enough," he replied, not wanting to burden Shiro with his thoughts.

"I've been thinking about our tour of Hanamachi yesterday," Shiro said, setting down his chopsticks and leaning back in his chair. "I'm sure you noticed how prosperous it is. The people live without fear, and the town thrives because of the protection I offer. I trust you saw the benefits of my methods?"

Wakamono hesitated, glancing down at his plate. Shiro's words made sense on the surface—the town did appear to be flourishing, at least in the wealthier districts. But Red Mist's warnings echoed in his mind, and the sight of the struggling farmers at the edge of town was not so easily forgotten.

"Yes... but," Wakamono started, choosing his words carefully, "Red Mist pointed out that not everyone is as fortunate. The poorer areas... they seemed to be suffering."

Shiro waved a hand dismissively, a slight smile playing on his lips. "That's the natural order of things, Wakamono. There will always be those who struggle more than others. My duty is to maintain peace and ensure that the majority are protected. If a few must fall by the wayside, that's the price we pay for stability. The strong must rule, and the weak must serve."

Wakamono didn't respond immediately, feeling torn. He admired Shiro's strength and the sense of order he had brought to Hanamachi, but Red Mist had always taught him that the role of a Kōken was to protect everyone, not just the most fortunate.

Before he could voice his doubts, the doors to the dining hall burst open, and a disheveled currier stumbled inside, breathless and clearly in a hurry.

"Lord Shiro! There's an attack—kappa, from the river! They're wreaking havoc on the farms!" the currier panted, his face pale with fear.

Wakamono shot up from his seat, his heart racing at the thought of the townspeople in danger. "We should go!" he urged, already reaching for his katana.

Shiro, however, remained seated, calmly sipping his tea as though the news were nothing more than a mild inconvenience. He raised an eyebrow at the currier's intrusion, but made no move to rise.

"Calm yourself," Shiro said coolly. "There's no need to rush. The kappa will still be there when we arrive. Besides, I haven't finished my breakfast."

The currier stood awkwardly at the door, glancing between Shiro and Wakamono, clearly unsure of what to do. Wakamono, meanwhile, stared at Shiro in disbelief.

"Shiro, we can't just sit here!" Wakamono protested, his voice filled with urgency. "People are in danger!"

Shiro sighed and leaned back in his chair, picking up a piece of fruit and popping it into his mouth. "The townspeople should know how to deal with minor pests like the kappa. Let them handle it for a while longer. We'll leave when I'm ready."

Wakamono felt a surge of frustration, his hands clenching into fists. He couldn't understand how Shiro could be so indifferent to the suffering of the people he claimed to protect. This wasn't how Red Mist would have handled the situation. She would have been out the door the moment she heard of the attack.

The currier shifted again, clearly aware of the tension in the room. "Lord Shiro... the kappa have already killed a few farmers. The people are begging for your help."

Shiro glanced at the currier, his expression unreadable. For a moment, the room was silent, the only sound the soft clink of Shiro's chopsticks against his plate. Then, with an air of mild annoyance, he finally stood.

"Very well," he said with a casual wave of his hand. "Let's not keep the kappa waiting any longer."

Wakamono exhaled in relief, though he couldn't shake the anger simmering beneath the surface. As they left the dining hall and prepared to head to the farms, he couldn't help but wonder: was this the kind of leader Shiro had become? One who put his own comfort before the lives of those under his protection? And, was this kind of person he wanted to be?

As they exited the estate, Wakamono glanced back at the grand structure, his thoughts once again pulled in two directions. He had admired Shiro's strength, but now he couldn't help but question the cost of that strength.

With Shiro leading the way, they descended toward the farms, but the weight of doubt pressed heavier on Wakamono's shoulders with each step.

後見

The sun had risen higher by the time Shiro and Wakamono reached the outskirts of the village, the sounds of chaos growing louder with every step. Farmers shouted in panic, the clamor of livestock and the crashing of wooden carts filling the air. As they approached the fields, Wakamono's eyes widened in shock.

A group of grotesque creatures—each about the size of a small man, with green, scaly skin and elongated limbs—rampaged through the crops. Their large, saucer-like eyes gleamed with malice, and their mouths were twisted in grotesque grins. The kappa moved quickly, their hands gripping large cucumbers and crude, makeshift weapons. Each had a small, water-filled depression on the top of their heads, shimmering like a crown of sorts.

The villagers were powerless against the onslaught. A few brave farmers tried to fend off the kappa with pitchforks, but the creatures dodged their strikes with unnatural agility, knocking them to the ground and beating them with both cucumbers and clubs. Others, seeing no hope of stopping the creatures, fled toward the safety of their homes.

Wakamono instinctively reached for his katana, his heart racing. "Shiro, we have to help them!"

Shiro, however, seemed unbothered by the chaos unfolding before them. He surveyed the scene with a calculating gaze, his lips curling into a faint smirk. "Patience, Wakamono. There's no need to rush into this. Let the kappa amuse themselves for a bit longer."

Wakamono stared at him in disbelief. "Amuse themselves? They're killing people!"

Shiro shrugged, seemingly indifferent. "A few casualties were inevitable. But look around, Wakamono." He gestured toward the fleeing farmers. "The ones who survive will be stronger for it and be reminded of my importance. As for the ones who don't... well, there's more land to be divided."

As if on cue, one of the farmers—a burly man wielding a shovel—was knocked to the ground by a kappa. The creature screeched with laughter, beating him mercilessly with its club. Blood spattered the ground as the man struggled to rise, only to be struck down again.

Wakamono clenched his fists, fury rising in his chest. This wasn't how a Kōken was supposed to act. Shiro's cold detachment in the face of suffering was incomprehensible to him. He had to do something.

"I'm not going to stand here and watch this," Waka-mono growled, drawing his katana and sprinting toward the nearest kappa.

Shiro chuckled behind him but made no move to stop him. "As you wish. But remember, Wakamono, power is not just about rushing into battle. It's about discipline, self-control," Shiro called out, mockingly.

Wakamono ignored him, focusing on the task at hand. He closed the distance between himself and the kappa in seconds, raising his katana high. The creature turned just in time to see the blade descending, and with a sharp hiss, it jumped backward, narrowly avoiding the strike.

Wakamono pressed the attack, slashing at the kappa's legs and torso. The creature moved with unnerving speed, ducking and weaving as it tried to counter Wakamono's strikes. But it was no match for Wakamono's training. He noticed the water glistening on the top of the creature's head—its weak point.

With a calculated feint, Wakamono brought his blade down, knocking the kappa off balance. As the creature staggered, Wakamono struck the water on its head with the flat of his katana. The water splashed to the ground, and the kappa let out a groan of agony, collapsing in a limp heap.

Wakamono allowed himself a moment of satisfaction before turning to face the next kappa. But as he scanned the battlefield, he saw that Shiro had already made his move.

Shiro strode into the fray with an air of casual dominance, his movements precise and deadly. His katana flashed through the air, cutting down kappa with brutal efficiency. There was no hesitation in his strikes, no mercy in his eyes. One by one, the creatures fell before him, their bodies crumpling to the ground as blood and smashed cucumbers spread over the soil.

Wakamono felt a chill run down his spine as he watched. Shiro wasn't just defeating the kappa—he was annihilating them. The villagers looked on in horror as their supposed protector cut through the creatures without remorse, his blade leaving a trail of carnage in its wake.

Eventually, Shiro stood before the last remaining kappa, a sneer of disdain on his face. The creature, realizing it was outmatched, tried to flee, but Shiro was faster. He kicked the kappa to the ground, spilling the water from its head, and in one swift motion, decapitated it with a single, clean stroke.

Shiro sheathed his katana, his expression unreadable as he turned to Wakamono. "And that, Wakamono, is how you deal with pests."

Wakamono was still catching his breath, his mind reeling from the brutality of what he had just witnessed. "You... you didn't have to kill them all," he said quietly.

Shiro raised an eyebrow, as if surprised by the comment. "Of course I did. They were a threat to the town. A leader must be willing to do whatever is necessary to protect his people."

"But the people..." Wakamono gestured to the cowering farmers. "They're terrified of you."

Shiro's lips curled into a cold smile. "Fear is a powerful tool, Wakamono. It ensures obedience. It keeps people in line."

Wakamono looked at the bodies of the fallen kappa, the blood-soaked ground, and the horrified faces of the villagers. He had thought that being a Kōken meant protecting people, but Shiro's methods... they were ruthless, even cruel.

Shiro placed a hand on Wakamono's shoulder, his voice low and commanding. "You did well today. But you must understand, Wakamono—power is not about mercy. It's about dominance. And that means making hard choices."

Wakamono didn't respond, his mind swirling with conflicting thoughts. He had finally taken action, as he had wanted to, but at what cost? The brutality of Shiro's methods left a bitter taste in his mouth, and for the first time, he began to question the path that lay before him.

As they turned to leave, Shiro addressed the remaining farmers with cold authority. "The land of those who died today will be redistributed among you.

But your tribute to the estate will increase to reflect the expanded plots. Remember, I protect those who remain loyal."

The farmers nodded, their faces pale and drawn, too afraid to protest.

Wakamono followed Shiro back toward the estate, his heart heavy with doubt. The thrill of battle had faded, replaced by the harsh reality of Shiro's rule.

As Wakamono and Shiro walked, the late afternoon sun casting long shadows across the cobbled streets, Shiro spoke at length about power and control. His voice was calm, almost casual, as if he were explaining the simple rules of life rather than the darker philosophies that governed his rule.

"You see, Wakamono," Shiro began, gesturing toward the town with a sweep of his hand, "people are creatures of habit. They need structure, guidance... and yes, sometimes a firm hand to keep them in line. Fear is an efficient motivator, and when people are afraid, they tend to obey. They will offer you their loyalty, even their admiration, because deep down, they know that the alternative is chaos."

Wakamono listened, his eyes focused on the ground as Shiro's words sank in. His thoughts were a jumble, conflicting emotions swirling through his mind. He had seen the terror in the farmers' eyes back in the village. The way they cowered before Shiro, their so-called protector, was unsettling. Was that what it meant to be a leader? To command fear and obedience at the expense of kindness and compassion?

As they passed through the marketplace, the bustling crowds parted to allow them through. People hurried to avoid crossing Shiro's path, casting furtive glances at him from the corners of their eyes. There was fear in their gazes, as Shiro had said. But as Wakamono observed them more closely, he noticed something else—a flicker of resentment, of quiet defiance. Some of the people looked at Shiro not with respect or fear, but with contempt.

Wakamono furrowed his brow, his thoughts drifting to Red Mist. She had always spoken of control in a different way—control over one's emotions, one's actions, and above all, one's sense of duty. Her lessons had always emphasized self-discipline, the idea that a Kōken was a guardian, not a ruler. To her, the true strength of a Kōken came not from domination over others but from mastery over oneself.

Shiro's philosophy, on the other hand, seemed to center around tyranny, about bending others to his will. Wakamono had seen the result of that philosophy today, in the bodies of the dead kappa, in the terrified faces of the farmers.

"It's not just about strength," Shiro continued, oblivious to Wakamono's growing unease. "It's about perception. People need to believe that you are their only hope, their savior. Once they see you as the one thing standing between them and disaster, they will do anything to keep you in power. You become indispensable."

Wakamono nodded absentmindedly, his mind racing. Was that what a Kōken was supposed to be? Indispensable? He thought back to his training with Red Mist, her lessons about humility and service, about protecting the weak without expecting anything in return. She had never sought to control anyone; she had only ever sought to help, to make the world a better place, one small step at a time.

But Shiro's words were tempting. The power he wielded, the influence he commanded—it was undeniable. Wakamono had grown up in a small, humble farm village, where survival was a daily struggle. The idea of being in control, of being able to shape the world around him, was alluring. He could do so much, he thought, if he had the power that Shiro possessed. He could protect his family, his home. He could ensure that no one ever had to suffer or live in fear.

But at what cost?

"You're thinking too hard," Shiro remarked, his tone light but his eyes sharp. "I can see the wheels turning in your head, Wakamono. You're wondering if Red Mist has taught you everything, aren't you? Whether there's more to being a Kōken than the ideals she clings to."

Wakamono hesitated, unsure of how to respond. He didn't want to betray Red Mist, but there was a kernel of truth in Shiro's words. He had begun to wonder if the Kōken ideals were enough, if they were too rigid, too... naïve.

Shiro smirked, as if reading Wakamono's thoughts. "I'm not saying she's wrong about everything. But the world isn't as simple as honor and duty. People are unpredictable, selfish. If you want to protect them, you need to be willing to do what's necessary. Sometimes that means taking control, even if they resent you for it."

They reached the entrance to the estate, the towering gates creaking open as the guards bowed in respect. As they entered the courtyard, Wakamono glanced back at the town one last time. The people still moved about their lives, but the weight of Shiro's rule was palpable in the air, like a heavy fog that never lifted.

He couldn't help but wonder if there was another way. Could power really be the answer to everything? Or was Shiro leading him down a path that would only end in darkness?

As they walked into the estate, Wakamono resolved to speak with Red Mist again. He needed to hear her perspective, to understand what she thought of Shiro's philosophy. There had to be more to being a Kōken than this.

But deep down, a quiet voice whispered that he was already starting to see the appeal of Shiro's vision. Why not make the most of his strength? He could do it differently than Shiro. He could be a merciful, honorable leader.

後見

Wakamono found Red Mist in the courtyard, seated on a wooden bench beneath the shade of an ancient tree. She was meditating, her posture straight and calm as always, but there was a heaviness to her presence that Wakamono hadn't noticed before. Her eyes were closed, her breathing steady, as if she were trying to center herself in the midst of something unsettling.

He hesitated for a moment before approaching, not wanting to disturb her, but the thoughts swirling in his mind needed release. The day's events had left him conflicted, and he needed to hear her perspective. He needed to understand what she saw in Shiro that was so dangerous.

"Red Mist," he called softly as he neared, his voice hesitant.

Her eyes opened slowly, and she regarded him with a calm, measured gaze. "You've returned," she said simply, though her eyes hinted at a deeper concern.

Wakamono sat beside her, resting his hands on his knees. He could feel the tension in his body, the weight of the day's encounters pressing down on him. "We went to the farms near the river," he began, recounting the kappa attack and how Shiro had dealt with it.

Red Mist listened in silence as he spoke. When he finished, there was a long pause. She seemed to be choosing her words carefully, as if deciding how much to say.

"Shiro's methods haven't changed," she said finally, her voice quiet but firm. "He acts with force and precision, but without compassion. To him, people are pawns, not individuals with lives and families. He sees them as tools to further his power."

Wakamono frowned. "But... he's protecting the town. They're safer with him in control, aren't they? I saw how the farmers looked at him. They were afraid, yes, but they also seemed... relieved."

Red Mist shook her head slowly. "Fear may bring temporary obedience, but it doesn't inspire loyalty. And it doesn't create lasting peace. What Shiro has built here is fragile, Wakamono. It's built on fear, not trust. Eventually, fear will turn to resentment. And resentment... it breeds rebellion."

Her words struck a chord in him, but he couldn't shake the images of the wealthy streets, the prosperous market, the grand estate. "But the town is thriving," he argued, feeling the need to push back. "I saw it. The wealth, the order. Shiro's brought stability to a place that used to be overrun by spirits and beasts. Isn't that what we're supposed to do as Kōken? Bring order and protect people?"

"Protection can't come at the cost of people's freedom," Red Mist replied, her tone sharpening. "We are Kōken, yes, but our duty is to serve, not to rule. We protect because it is our calling, not because it gives us power over others. Shiro's forgotten that."

She turned to face him fully now, her gaze intense. "I overheard something today while you were with Shiro," she continued, her voice lowering. "I disguised myself and mingled with the townspeople. There's unrest brewing, Wakamono. The people are nervous—restless. They know more Kōken have arrived, and they don't know whether to see us as a threat or as hope."

Wakamono's brow furrowed. "A revolt?"

Red Mist nodded. "It hasn't fully formed yet, but there are whispers. The lower classes are suffering, and they're beginning to blame Shiro. They don't know that we're here to help, not to reinforce his rule. They're afraid that more Kōken means more oppression."

Her words settled over him like a heavy weight. Wakamono had seen the glances of contempt from the villagers, but he hadn't understood the full extent of their dissatisfaction. Now, he was starting to piece it together. The wealth and prosperity Shiro had brought to the town hadn't reached everyone. Beneath the surface of order and stability, there was resentment bubbling.

"But... Shiro doesn't seem worried," Wakamono said, recalling how casually Shiro had dismissed the idea of unrest. "He's confident that he has control."

"Of course he is," Red Mist replied. "Shiro's pride is his greatest flaw. He believes his power is unshakable, that no one can challenge him. But pride blinds him to the reality of what's happening. The people are afraid of him, yes, but fear isn't enough to keep them in check forever. You know what happens when you back a wild beast into a corner."

She leaned forward slightly, her gaze softening as she looked at Wakamono. "You need to be careful," she warned, her voice filled with concern. "Shiro is trying to pull you into his way of thinking. He sees your potential, and he wants to shape you in his image. But his path... it only leads to darkness."

Wakamono shifted uncomfortably. He didn't want to believe that Shiro's path was so dangerous. Shiro had shown him power, yes, but there was something about it that was undeniably appealing. The ability to shape the world, to control it—wasn't that what they were supposed to do as Kōken? Protect the people by keeping them in line, by ensuring order?

But Red Mist's words echoed in his mind. *Authority is not our purpose. Service is.*

He looked down at his hands, uncertainty gnawing at him. "I... I don't know what to think anymore," he admitted. "Shiro's shown me things I've never considered before. And maybe... maybe there's some truth in what he says. The world is harsh, isn't it? Maybe taking control is necessary. Maybe we can show him how to lead more mercifully."

Red Mist sighed, her expression pained. "The world *is* harsh, Wakamono. But control through fear will only make it harsher. Don't let Shiro's vision cloud your own. You must remain true to yourself, to the values of the Kōken. If you stray from that path, you will lose more than just your way. You will lose who you are."

She stood, her silhouette dark against the fading light of the courtyard. "We must tread carefully now," she said, her tone serious. "Shiro's time here is running out, whether he knows it or not. And if we're not careful, we'll be caught in the storm that's coming."

Wakamono nodded, though his mind was still torn. Red Mist's words made sense, but Shiro's vision was powerful, tempting. He had seen the prosperity Shiro had brought to the town and the wealth he had accumulated, and he couldn't deny its appeal.

As Red Mist left him alone in the courtyard, Wakamono stared up at the night sky, the stars twinkling above him like distant, unreachable truths.

Which path was the right one? And which would he follow?

8
八

RED MIST AWOKE TO the sound of a faint creak—the
kind of sound that would be imperceptible to most,
but her honed instincts had long ago attuned her
senses to even the subtlest disturbances. Her eyes
snapped open, her body instantly alert, though she
remained still. In the darkness of her room, the shadows stretched long and deep, concealing whoever—or
whatever—had dared enter.

She heard the whisper of footsteps. The assassin
was good, careful. But not careful enough.

A soft *swish* cut through the air as a blade descended
toward her bed. Red Mist rolled swiftly to the side, her
body a blur of movement as she avoided the deadly
strike. The blade cut into the bedding, but her as-
sailant had no time to recover. In an instant, Red
Mist was on her feet, her katana in hand, the steel
glinting coldly in the moonlight that filtered through
the narrow window.

The room was small and dark, leaving little space
for error. The assassin lunged again, aiming for her

chest, but Red Mist parried the blow with ease, the clash of their weapons reverberating in the stillness of the night. As their blades locked, she saw the face of her attacker—masked, emotionless. A professional.

But it wasn't just one. A second assassin emerged from the shadows, flanking her. Red Mist disengaged and spun, narrowly avoiding a dagger aimed for her back. She leapt toward the far corner of the room, flipping over a low table as the second assassin swiped at her legs. The room was cramped, the tight quarters offering no room for elaborate maneuvers, but Red Mist thrived in such conditions. Her movements were fluid, calculated, and deliberate, her mind racing as she planned each step ahead.

The second assassin moved in for another strike, but Red Mist sidestepped and slammed the hilt of her katana into his ribs with a force that sent him staggering. He collided with the wall, gasping for breath. The first assassin, undeterred, swung his blade at her again. Red Mist ducked low and drove her knee into his midsection, knocking the wind out of him. He dropped his weapon, and with a swift, controlled motion, she flipped him onto his back and pressed her blade to his throat.

But it wasn't over.

A third figure slipped through the open door. This one, larger and more imposing, held a long naginata. Red Mist released her first opponent and turned to face the newcomer, her stance shifting to accommodate the new threat. The naginata wielder wasted no time, thrusting forward with practiced precision. Red Mist parried with her katana, but the longer weapon's reach kept her at bay.

She glanced at the door, realizing that her best chance was to get outside, into the open where she would have more room to maneuver. She feinted left, then dashed right, evading the assassin's next thrust and using the momentary distraction to kick the door open. The fresh night air hit her as she leaped outside, the assassins following close behind.

The courtyard was bathed in moonlight, casting long shadows from the walls and trees. Red Mist felt a surge of energy as her feet touched the open ground. Here, in the open space, she could fully unleash her skills.

The naginata-wielding assassin charged at her, but Red Mist was ready. She sidestepped his initial thrust and swept her katana upward, slicing the polearm in two with a single, precise cut. The assassin, momentarily stunned, had no chance to react before Red Mist disarmed him, twisting his wrist and sending the remnants of the weapon clattering to the ground. In one fluid motion, she incapacitated him with a well-placed strike to the back of his neck, sending him crumpling to the ground, unconscious.

She turned her attention to the remaining two assassins, who had regrouped and were advancing cautiously. Red Mist's gaze flicked between them, her breathing steady. They were good, trained to kill, but she had the advantage now.

The first assassin attacked with a flurry of strikes, but Red Mist deflected each blow with ease, her katana moving like a silver streak in the moonlight. She waited for an opening, then countered with a swift upward slash, grazing his arm and forcing him to retreat. The second assassin lunged at her from behind, but Red Mist anticipated the move. She spun on her heel, sweeping her leg out in a low arc and knocking him off his feet. He rested motionless after his skull bounced off the hard ground.

With all three assassins disarmed and incapacitated, Red Mist stood tall, her katana gleaming in the moonlight as she surveyed the scene. The courtyard was silent once more, save for the labored breathing of the defeated assassins.

She stared down at them, her mind racing. This attack wasn't random. It was well-coordinated, precise. These assassins were professionals, sent by someone with a clear objective. And the timing...

Her eyes narrowed as realization dawned. The timing of the assassination attempt had coincided perfectly with the growing unrest in the town.

Shiro.

He had known. He had known about the unrest and had waited until the perfect moment to strike, using the chaos as a cover for this attempt on her life. Red Mist felt a cold fury settle in her chest. Shiro's influence was more dangerous than she had anticipated.

As she sheathed her katana, her thoughts turned to Wakamono. She had to warn him—there was no telling what Shiro had planned next.

Without wasting another moment, Red Mist strode across the courtyard, her heart pounding with a new sense of urgency.

後見

Red Mist stormed into Wakamono's quarters, her expression sharp, her katana still unsheathed. Wakamono, startled from his rest, sat up quickly.

"What's wrong?" he asked, his voice still thick with sleep.

"There was an assassination attempt," she said curtly, pacing to the window to glance out. "Three of them—professionals. Shiro is behind it, or at the very least, he's aware of it."

Wakamono's eyes widened. "Shiro? That doesn't make sense. He's..."

Red Mist spun around, cutting him off. "Shiro is not who you think he is, Wakamono. He's more dangerous than we realized. We need to leave now, before things get worse."

Wakamono hesitated, his mind reeling. The events of the last few days—the luxurious estate, the kappa attack, Shiro's seemingly calm demeanor—it all conflicted with what Red Mist was saying. But he could see the urgency in her eyes, the seriousness in her tone.

"What should we do?" he asked, standing and reaching for his weapons.

"Pack light. We don't have time. We need to leave the estate immediately before Shiro discovers the attempt failed, if he doesn't already know. He has the advantage here. We need to regroup and come up with a plan to remove him."

Wakamono began hastily gathering his gear, his mind racing with questions. Why would Shiro send assassins after Red Mist? Wasn't he their ally, despite their differences in philosophy? And yet, deep down, he couldn't ignore the growing doubts in his mind.

Just as Wakamono finished strapping on his katana, a thunderous sound shook the air. Shouts and crashes echoed from beyond the walls, like the tide of an approaching storm.

Red Mist tensed. "No..."

They moved swiftly to the window, peering out into the dark. Through the dim moonlight, they could see movement at the estate's gate—figures clashing, shadows weaving through the open space. A crowd was gathering, torches flickering in the distance.

"It's happening," Red Mist muttered. "The rebellion."

Wakamono's heart sank. The words of the townspeople flashed through his mind—the whispers of unrest, of discontent festering beneath the surface. He'd heard it, felt it, but he hadn't realized how close the people had come to breaking. Now, it was too late.

The gates of Shiro's estate were wide open, and a surge of angry townspeople flooded in. Their faces, twisted with anger and desperation, were illuminated by the flickering torchlight. Some held crude weapons—shovels, rakes, and wooden clubs—while others simply charged with bare fists, their rage fueling them.

"They've broken through," Red Mist said, turning to Wakamono. "We have to move, now!"

Just as she spoke, the sound of a loud horn echoed through the night. Shiro's guards scrambled to respond, rushing from the barracks and taking positions near the main courtyard, their armor clanking as they moved. The rebellion had begun, and the estate had become a battlefield.

Red Mist grabbed Wakamono by the arm and pulled him toward the door. "We're not getting caught in this. Stick close."

They moved quickly through the halls of the estate, trying to avoid the growing chaos outside. The sounds of fighting grew louder, and Red Mist knew it was only a matter of time before they were caught in the middle of it.

As they rounded a corner, Red Mist paused, pulling Wakamono back into the shadows. A group of Shiro's guards ran past, their weapons drawn, heading toward the gates to confront the mob. The tension in the air was palpable, and the atmosphere was heavy with the threat of violence.

"We're not going to make it out unnoticed," Red Mist whispered, her eyes scanning the hallway for an escape route. "We need to find another way."

Suddenly, a deafening crash echoed from the front of the estate. The townspeople had reached the inner walls and were forcing their way in, smashing through the doors and windows with whatever they could find. Shiro's guards, overwhelmed by the sheer number of attackers, struggled to hold them back.

Wakamono clenched his fists. "We can't just leave them. These people..."

"We're not here to take sides in this rebellion," Red Mist said firmly. "Our mission is Shiro, and if we don't get out of here now, we'll be caught in the crossfire."

Before they could move, the door to the main courtyard burst open, and a group of rebels spilled into the estate. Their faces were wild with rage, their eyes burning with fury as they charged toward the guards. The clash of steel and the shouts of battle filled the air, and chaos erupted all around them.

Suddenly, the doors to the great hall were thrown open, and Shiro appeared. He stood at the top of the steps leading down to the courtyard, his posture commanding as he surveyed the chaos below. For a moment, the crowd seemed to pause, their attention shifting to the man they had come to overthrow.

Shiro's face was impassive, his expression unreadable as he looked down at the people who had once worshipped him. He said nothing, but his mere presence was enough to reignite the fury in the crowd. The rebels surged forward again, shouting his name with venom.

Red Mist and Wakamono watched from the shadows, hidden from view as Shiro descended the steps. His guards flanked him, forming a protective barrier around their master. But even they seemed uncertain, glancing nervously at the approaching mob.

Shiro raised his hand, and the crowd fell silent. His voice, when he spoke, was cold and commanding. "You come here with fire and fury, thinking you can topple me. But you forget—I am the one who saved you. I am the one who gave you prosperity, safety."

The crowd murmured angrily, but no one dared speak out.

Shiro's gaze swept across the sea of faces. "You owe me your lives. Everything you have, everything you are, is because of me."

As the tension in the courtyard reached its breaking point, the fragile silence shattered. A single voice in the crowd rang out, defiant and desperate. "You are no savior! You're a tyrant!"

The words acted like a spark to dry tinder, igniting the crowd into a furious frenzy. The mob surged forward, armed with crude weapons and burning rage. Shiro's guards, though well-trained, were unprepared for the sheer number of rebels. For every strike they made, two more villagers pressed forward, their determination outweighing their fear.

Wakamono's hand tightened on the hilt of his katana as the chaos unfolded. He had seen fights before—against beasts, spirits, and dark creatures—but this was different. These were people, desperate and angry, fighting for their freedom.

At first, the guards held the line, parrying blows and pushing the rebels back. But then, one of the guards fell—a well-aimed rock to the temple sending him crumpling to the ground. The rebels seized the moment, swarming over the fallen guard and breaking through the line. The remaining guards faltered, overwhelmed by the sudden surge.

Shiro, who had been watching with that cold, calculating smile, frowned. His eyes narrowed as he saw the tide of battle turning against his men.

"Pathetic," he muttered under his breath.

Calmly and without hesitation, Shiro stepped forward, drawing his own katana with a fluid grace that sent a chill down Wakamono's spine. For a moment, Wakamono felt a flicker of admiration for Shiro's skill—his movements were precise, his posture flawless—but that admiration was quickly drowned out by the horror of what came next.

"I suppose I should be thankful, really," Shiro shouted toward the writhing mass of chaos. "It will be much easier to exterminate you all here, together, than to hunt you down individually."

Shiro moved like a shadow through the crowd, his blade flashing in the torchlight. With each strike, rebels fell, their makeshift weapons clattering to the ground. Shiro's katana sliced through the mob with a ruthless efficiency, and the once-frantic rebellion began to falter under the weight of his violence.

Through the madness of sprayed blood and severed limbs, some townspeople were able to reach the main hall. Thrusting their torches upon it, flames rapidly engulfed the building.

The remnants of lost lives splattered across the cobblestones, the cries of the wounded and dying filling the air. The mob, who moments ago had been so certain of their victory, now found themselves retreating, their will crumbling in the face of Shiro's unrelenting assault.

Wakamono could hardly breathe as he watched. This wasn't a battle—it was a slaughter. The people who had once looked to Shiro as their protector were being cut down like animals. Crimson stained the courtyard, reflecting the flickering light of the burning hall, and the stench of death mixed with the smoke that clouded the courtyard.

"Do you see now, Wakamono?" Shiro's voice carried over the dying cries. "This is how you maintain order. Not through mercy, but through strength. Through fear and brutality."

Wakamono's mind raced. Shiro's words echoed in his head, but they didn't make sense. This wasn't protection. This wasn't the path of the Kōken.

Red Mist, standing beside Wakamono, could see the turmoil in his eyes. She grabbed his arm.

"We can't let this continue," she whispered, her voice tense but steady. "Shiro has lost himself. If we don't stop him now, he'll kill them all."

Wakamono's heart pounded in his chest. He looked at the courtyard, at the blood-soaked ground, at the bodies of the villagers lying motionless. His hand clenched around the hilt of his katana. Everything Red Mist had taught him, everything he believed in, was being tested in this moment.

Their movement gained Shiro's attention as fleeing townspeople scattered.

"How did it come to this?" Wakamono asked, his voice barely audible. "How did he become this?"

Red Mist's expression hardened. "Shiro believes that power is the only way to protect people, but all it's done is corrupt him. He's forgotten what it means to be Kōken. He cannot be saved."

They both turned their attention back to the courtyard, where Shiro stood amidst the bodies of the fallen, his katana gleaming in the firelight. His expression was unreadable, but the coldness in his eyes was unmistakable.

"This," Shiro said, his voice carrying a terrifying calmness, "is what it means to rule!"

Wakamono's stomach turned at Shiro's words. This wasn't protection. This was ruthless tyranny and murder. And it was wrong.

"I'm ready," Wakamono said, his voice filled with a newfound resolve.

Red Mist nodded, her grip tightening on her own blade.

Without another word, they stepped forward, ready to put an end to the bloodshed.

9
九

THE COURTYARD, NOW EERILY silent after the rebellion's violent suppression, stood under a blood-red
sky. The smoke from the fires drifted through the air,
carrying with it the stench of burnt wood and spilled
blood. Shiro stood in the center, his katana sheathed
but his posture tense, as if he knew the final battle
was inevitable. Red Mist and Wakamono approached
him, their footsteps echoing on the stone ground, the
weight of what was about to happen heavy in the air.

Shiro's eyes flicked between the two, but they lingered on Wakamono. There was a glimmer of something in his gaze—curiosity, perhaps even admiration.
But behind it, there was also arrogance, a certainty
that this battle would end on his terms.

"You came all this way, Red Mist," Shiro said with a
cool smile, "but for what? To challenge me? To what
end? Look around you." He gestured to the smoldering ruins, the fallen townspeople, the scattered bodies
of the rebels and guards. "This is the world we live in.
A world where strength is the only law that matters."

Red Mist's face was set in stone, her eyes hard with determination. "This isn't strength, Shiro. This is weakness. Weakness of the mind to temptation, greed, and pride. You've lost your way."

Shiro's smile widened, but his eyes showed only malevolence. "I've found the only way that works. The world is changing, and if you're not changing with it, you'll be a victim of it. We can reshape this town—this entire land and beyond. Together. To the benefit of all."

Wakamono felt the weight of Shiro's words, the temptation seeping into his bones. He had seen the power Shiro commanded, the respect and fear he garnered. And for a moment, a flicker of doubt stirred in his heart. Could Shiro be right? Could control truly be the way to protect the people, to keep them safe?

But then he remembered the blood in the streets, the faces of the farmers Shiro had so casually dismissed. And he remembered the values Red Mist had taught him—the values of honor, restraint, and protecting the weak. His doubt was swallowed by resolve.

"You're wrong, Shiro," Wakamono said, his voice steady. "This isn't what makes one strong. It's being the person you must be, in spite of your desires."

Shiro's smile faded, replaced by something colder, more dangerous. His hand moved to the hilt of his katana. "Then let's see if you've learned anything from your master, boy."

With a swift motion, Shiro unsheathed his blade. In the blink of an eye, he lunged at Red Mist, the speed of his strike forcing her to parry with barely a moment to spare. The clash of steel rang out across the courtyard, and the battle began.

Wakamono drew his own katana, rushing to Red Mist's side. Together, they moved in sync, their blades slicing through the air as they engaged Shiro. But Shiro was fast—faster than either of them had anticipated. His strikes were precise, his movements fluid, as if he had been waiting for this fight his entire life. Of course, he must have known the Kōken would come for him, eventually.

Shiro pressed the attack, his katana flashing like lightning. Red Mist parried his strikes with skill, her movements graceful and efficient, but it was clear that Shiro had gained an edge. His technique was masterful, each swing of his sword calculated to exploit any opening.

Wakamono, determined not to fall behind, launched his own attacks. He moved with a speed and agility that surprised even himself, the training Red Mist had instilled in him coming to the forefront. He weaved between Shiro's strikes, delivering quick, sharp blows of his own, testing Shiro's defenses.

For a moment, it seemed like they had the upper hand. But then, Shiro shifted his stance, his blade spinning in a rapid arc. With a powerful swing, he knocked Wakamono back, sending him stumbling across the courtyard. Before Wakamono could recover, Shiro pivoted and engaged Red Mist, the force of his strikes pushing her toward the edge of the courtyard.

Wakamono struggled to his feet, his vision blurred from the impact. He watched as Red Mist parried another of Shiro's brutal attacks, her arms shaking from the effort. Shiro was relentless, pressing her back step by step, his grin growing as he sensed her weakening resolve.

"Is this all you have?" Shiro taunted, his voice dripping with scorn. "You talk about honor, about protecting people, but all it does is make you weak!"

With a desperate surge of strength, Red Mist spun her katana in a defensive arc, forcing Shiro to retreat a step. But she was breathing heavily now, the weight of the fight clearly wearing her down. Shiro, however, looked as if he had barely broken a sweat.

Wakamono, shaking off the dizziness, gripped his katana and rushed forward. He couldn't let Red Mist fight alone. He joined the fray once more, his blade striking out at Shiro in a flurry of determined blows.

But Shiro was ready. With a swift parry, he deflected Wakamono's attack and countered with a brutal slash that sent sparks flying from Wakamono's blade. Wakamono barely managed to block the next strike, but its force sent him staggering back again.

"You have potential, Wakamono," Shiro said, his voice almost casual as he deflected another strike. "You've learned well from Red Mist, but she's holding you back."

Wakamono's breath was ragged, but he refused to falter. "You're wrong. She's shown me the true path."

Shiro's eyes glinted dangerously. "Has she? Or has she just chained you to her outdated ideals?"

The battle paused, the three combatants circling each other warily. Shiro's gaze fixed on Wakamono, and for the first time since the fight began, his tone softened, almost persuasive.

"Think about it, Wakamono," Shiro said, his voice low and tempting. "You've seen what I can do. Together, we could be unstoppable. You could have power, wealth, respect. You wouldn't have to live in the shadows, bound by the old ways. You could help me reshape this world, bring order to the chaos. Isn't that what you want?"

Wakamono hesitated. The power Shiro offered was tempting—so tempting. For a moment, the weight of the katana in his hand felt like a burden rather than a tool of protection. He looked at Red Mist, who met his gaze with a silent plea, her eyes filled with concern.

But then Wakamono remembered the people of the town, the ones Shiro had crushed without a second thought. He remembered the farmers, the rebellion, and the blood that stained Shiro's hands. No. This wasn't what he wanted.

"I'll never join you," Wakamono said, his voice firm.

Shiro's expression hardened, and the tension in the courtyard snapped like a taut string.

"Then you'll fall like the rest," Shiro said coldly, raising his blade once more.

The battle was far from over.

In a flurry of movement, Shiro's blade cut through the pause.

Wakamono's breath came in short, shallow gasps as he fought to stay upright. His vision blurred, the edges of the world closing in as blood seeped from the deep gash Shiro had dealt him across his abdomen. He stumbled, his legs threatening to give way beneath him, but still, he gripped his katana with white-knuckled determination.

Red Mist, standing just a few feet away, saw the blood blooming across Wakamono's shirt and knew he didn't have much time. With a cry of fury, she lunged at Shiro, her blade slicing through the air with deadly precision. Shiro barely had time to raise his own weapon before Red Mist's attack came crashing down on him, the force of her strikes sending him stumbling back.

Wakamono's legs finally gave out, and he collapsed to one knee, his vision swimming. He watched helplessly as Red Mist fought on, her katana flashing like silver lightning as she pressed Shiro with everything she had. But Shiro was strong, and for every blow Red Mist landed, he countered with one of his own.

"It's good to see you letting go a little," Shiro sneered, his voice strained as he parried another strike. "But it will not be enough."

Red Mist didn't respond, her face a mask of calm fury. She swung again, her katana aimed at Shiro's side. The blade connected, slicing through Shiro's armor and drawing blood. Shiro let out a growl of pain, but his eyes flashed with fury as he retaliated. In a swift motion, he brought his own katana crashing down on Red Mist's shoulder before she could fully raise her defense.

The force of the blow sent Red Mist staggering back, but she didn't falter. Instead, she spun on her heel and delivered a sharp kick to Shiro's chest, sending him reeling. With a powerful thrust, Red Mist drove her katana forward, the blade plunging into Shiro's side.

Shiro gasped, his eyes wide with shock as the sword buried deep into his flesh. Blood poured from the wound, and for a moment, he faltered, clutching his side in pain. Red Mist withdrew her sword, her breath ragged but determined. She turned toward Waka-mono, who lay on the ground, his face pale and slick with sweat.

"Wakamono!" Red Mist rushed to his side, kneeling beside him. Her hands trembled as she searched through his pack. "The blade... Where's the healing blade?"

Wakamono's eyes fluttered open, his vision clouded with pain. He tried to speak, but no words came out, only a pained gasp.

Red Mist's heart raced as she frantically searched Wakamono's pack. The healing blade, their only hope to save him, wasn't there. Panic surged through her as she looked back at Wakamono's pale face.

"Where is it?" she whispered to herself, her voice tight with fear.

A dark laugh broke the tense silence, sending a chill down Red Mist's spine. She whipped around to see Shiro standing, blood dripping from his wound but his posture strong. In his hand, held aloft, was the healing blade.

"You're looking for this?" Shiro's voice was dripping with mockery, a twisted grin spreading across his face.

Red Mist's eyes widened in horror as she watched Shiro lift the healing blade to his own wound. Slowly, deliberately, he slid the blade into the gash she had inflicted, and as he withdrew it, the flesh began to knit itself back together, the wound closing almost as if it had never been there, leaving only the slightest scar.

"No!" Red Mist's voice cracked with fury as she surged to her feet, her katana raised.

Shiro laughed, a low, sinister sound, as he shifted his body, testing the newly healed skin. "You didn't think I'd let such a powerful tool go to waste, did you?" His eyes glinted with malice as he turned the healing blade over in his hand. "You've been holding out on me, Red Mist. This... this is something truly special. I had hoped the boy would share it with me on his own accord, but you would have never let that happen."

Red Mist's blood boiled as she charged at Shiro, her sword aimed at his heart. But Shiro was ready. With a swift movement, he parried her attack, the sound of steel clashing against steel echoing through the courtyard.

Wakamono lay on the ground, his strength fading fast as the darkness closed in around him. He could hear the sound of swords clashing, the grunts of effort and pain as Red Mist and Shiro fought for control of the blade. But he couldn't move. He couldn't help.

Shiro grinned wickedly as he taunted Red Mist. "This blade could make us unstoppable. We could live forever, Red Mist. Don't you see? We don't need to be bound by the old ways. With this power, we could rule everything."

Red Mist snarled in response, her strikes coming faster, harder, but Shiro deflected them with ease, the healing blade still held tightly in his hand.

Wakamono, fighting through the pain, felt a surge of desperation. He couldn't let Shiro win. Not like this. With a monumental effort, he forced himself to sit up, his vision swimming with darkness.

"Red Mist," he croaked, his voice barely above a whisper. "I... I can still fight."

Red Mist, locked in combat with Shiro, spared a glance at Wakamono, her heart breaking at the sight of him struggling to stay conscious. "Stay down, Wakamono!" she shouted, her voice laced with desperation. "You're too weak!"

But Wakamono wouldn't listen. With every ounce of strength he had left, he reached for his katana, gripping the hilt with trembling hands.

Shiro, seeing Wakamono's movement, smirked. "Oh? Still got some fight in you, boy? Let's see how long that lasts."

Red Mist, with renewed fury, launched herself at Shiro again, her strikes more vicious than ever. But Shiro, fully healed, seemed nearly unstoppable. He parried each attack with ease, a dark grin never leaving his face.

Wakamono's vision blurred as he staggered to his feet, his katana shaking in his hands. He knew he didn't have long. The wound in his abdomen burned like fire, and every step sent waves of agony through his body. But he wouldn't stop. He couldn't.

With a roar of effort, Wakamono charged at Shiro, his katana swinging in a desperate arc. Shiro, caught off guard, barely managed to block the strike and was forced to take his focus off of Red Mist.

Red Mist seized the opportunity. With a quick, fluid movement, she knocked the healing blade from Shiro's hand, sending it skittering across the stone floor.

Wakamono fell to his knees, the last of his strength leaving him as darkness closed in. The last thing he saw before the world went black was Red Mist standing over him, her eyes blazing with determination.

The courtyard was eerily quiet for a moment, save for the soft patter of wood on stone as the healing blade clattered to the ground. Red Mist's breath came in ragged gasps, her muscles burning from the intensity of the battle, but her eyes never left Shiro's. His smirk had faded, replaced with a cold, calculating stare as he assessed the situation.

"You're losing, Shiro," Red Mist said, her voice low and steady despite the exhaustion that gripped her. "It's over."

Shiro's lips twitched into a mocking grin. "Is it? Chikara?"

The use of her old name—the one she hadn't heard since their days as apprentices—hit her like a blow. Shiro's voice was smooth, almost affectionate, as he tried to summon memories of their shared past, but Red Mist's grip on her katana tightened. She couldn't allow herself to be distracted.

"I remember when we learned together, Chikara, more than just combat forms and dated ideals," Shiro continued, circling her slowly, his hand brushing the newly formed scar on his side. "We were the best. Both of us. But you... you were always the favorite. You were the one he gave a name to. A Kōken name. While I..." His voice hardened, bitter. "I left before he could 'bless' me with one."

"You left before you earned it," Red Mist shot back, her blade still poised. "Our master saw your impatience, your recklessness. You turned your back on everything we stood for."

Shiro's face twisted with rage, his eyes burning with jealousy. "And look where it's gotten me!" he shouted, gesturing to the opulent estate around them. "Power. Luxury. All of this is mine! While you're out there wandering from village to village, chasing down beasts and spirits like a dog."

"Like a Kōken," Red Mist corrected, her tone firm. "Serving and protecting. You've forgotten what that means."

Shiro's laughter was sharp, biting. "You've always been naïve. Power is the only thing that matters. Without it, you're nothing. You're no better than the people groveling at our feet." He took a step toward her, his katana raised again. "Join me, Chikara. Together, we could rule. The world could be ours. No one can stop the coming darkness. Let us embrace it."

Red Mist didn't falter. "I have no interest in ruling," she replied coldly, her eyes narrowing. "And I have no interest in the past. The Kōken aren't about power, Shiro. We're about honor. Something you've forgotten, if you ever had it."

Shiro lunged at her with a growl, his katana flashing in the dim light. Red Mist parried, her movements swift and precise, but she could feel the raw power behind his attacks. Shiro was fighting with everything he had now, his strikes fueled by rage and desperation.

For a moment, Red Mist was on the defensive, forced to block and dodge Shiro's relentless assault. He was strong—much stronger than he'd been during their training days—but his aggression left him exposed. She could see the cracks in his technique, the openings in his defenses as he overextended in his desire to overpower her.

"You were always so smug," Shiro hissed, his blade cutting through the air in a wild arc. "Always so sure of yourself. But look at you now, barely holding on."

Red Mist said nothing, her focus razor-sharp as she waited for her moment. Shiro's attacks were powerful, but they were becoming reckless. His emotions were clouding his judgment, and she could see it.

As Shiro brought his katana down in another sweeping strike, Red Mist sidestepped smoothly, her blade flashing out in a quick, precise motion. The tip of her sword sliced across Shiro's arm, drawing a deep cut.

Shiro snarled in pain, stumbling back. "You think you can win?!" he spat, his voice cracking with fury.

Red Mist didn't answer. She didn't need to. Instead, she pressed forward, her strikes measured and controlled, each one aimed to exploit the gaps in Shiro's defenses. Every time he swung too wide, too hard, she slipped inside his guard, landing small, precise blows that slowly wore him down.

Shiro's breathing grew ragged, his face twisted in frustration as he struggled to keep up. "Chikara!" he barked, trying to regain control, trying to rattle her. "I'm offering you a place at my side! Don't be a fool!"

But Red Mist was no longer listening. The vision she had seen—the city burning under Wakamono's rule, her death at his hand—was burned into her mind. She couldn't let the darkness take root, not in Wakamono, and not in herself.

With a final, powerful strike, Red Mist knocked Shiro's katana from his hand, sending it skittering across the courtyard. Shiro stumbled, his chest heaving as he tried to regain his balance, but Red Mist was already moving.

She closed the distance between them in an instant, her katana flashing as she delivered a swift, decisive blow to Shiro's leg. He collapsed to the ground with a howl of pain, clutching his wounded leg as blood pooled around him.

Red Mist stood over him, her katana raised, her breath coming in short gasps. She could end it now. She could strike him down and be done with it. But as she looked into Shiro's eyes—eyes that had once been filled with ambition and passion but were now clouded with bitterness and envy—she hesitated.

"Chikara..." Shiro rasped, his voice weak but defiant. "You... you can't kill me. We're the same, connected. You'll never be free of me."

Red Mist's eyes hardened. "No, Shiro. We were never the same."

She turned from him, rushing to Wakamono, who lay pale and still on the stone floor, grabbing the healing blade on her way. Kneeling beside him, she searched for and found a faint sign of life. With care, she slid the blade into and out of Wakamono's wound, watching as the flesh began to knit itself back together, the color slowly returning to his face.

Wakamono gasped, his eyes fluttering open as the healing blade did its work. He looked up at Red Mist, confusion and relief flooding his expression. "Red... Red Mist?" he croaked.

"It's all right," she whispered, her voice soft. "You're safe."

But behind her, Shiro stirred, his breathing ragged and uneven. Red Mist's body tensed. She knew that leaving him alive was a risk—one she couldn't afford to take.

Wakamono struggled to sit up, his strength slowly returning. He looked past Red Mist to where Shiro lay, broken and bleeding. "Red Mist... what are you...?"

She didn't answer. Slowly, she stood, turning to face her former comrade one last time.

Shiro's eyes were still defiant, even in his weakened state. "You can't... kill me," he rasped, his voice barely a whisper. "You don't... have the stomach for it."

For a moment, Red Mist said nothing. Then, with a single, fluid motion, she raised her katana and brought it down in a swift, merciful stroke.

The courtyard fell silent.

The battle was over. Shiro, once a proud and ambitious Kōken, lay dead at Red Mist's feet. Wakamono watched in stunned silence as Red Mist sheathed her blade, her expression unreadable. There was no victory in her eyes, only the weight of what had been done.

"Why?" Wakamono asked, his voice small.

Red Mist turned to him, her gaze steady but sad. "He was too dangerous to live. He left the path. Some people... can't be saved."

Wakamono swallowed, the reality of what had just happened sinking in. His mind was still racing with questions, but deep down, he knew she was right. Shiro had chosen his path long ago, and there had been no turning back for him.

As Red Mist helped Wakamono to his feet, the weight of their journey settled over them both. The battle with Shiro was over, but the scars it left behind would remain.

THE EARLY MORNING SUN had barely broken over the mountains when Red Mist and Wakamono walked through the gates of Shiro's estate for the last time. The town of Hanamachi was still quiet, the aftermath of the rebellion hanging in the air like a thick fog. Wakamono's steps were heavy, and though his wound had healed, the battle had left scars that would not so easily fade.

As they passed through the streets, the townspeople emerged from their homes, cautiously watching the pair of Kōken. Some looked relieved, others confused. And there were those who eyed them with fear, uncertain if their liberation from Shiro was a blessing or a curse. Shiro had been a harsh ruler, but he had kept them safe. Now, with him gone, the future seemed unclear, and the tension was palpable.

Wakamono glanced around, taking in the varied reactions of the townspeople. "They… they don't look happy," he said quietly, his voice laced with doubt.

"Some are relieved, but others will miss the security Shiro offered them," Red Mist replied, her voice calm but carrying the weight of her experience. "Fear can make people cling to even the worst kind of leader if it means protection from the unknown."

They made their way to the center of the town, where the elders had gathered, their faces lined with concern. A leader of the elders, an old man with a long white beard and deep-set eyes, approached them, bowing his head slightly in respect.

"Thank you," the elder said, though his tone was measured, cautious. "You've rid us of Shiro, but... what are we to do now?"

Red Mist looked at him steadily. "You'll need to govern yourselves," she said. "But I urge you—before you call upon another Kōken or seek help elsewhere, speak with your local temple. Many spirits can be dealt with through wisdom and negotiation. Violence should be the last resort."

The elder nodded, though there was a glint of skepticism in his eyes. "We'll do what we can," he replied, his gaze shifting toward the other elders, some of whom whispered among themselves. "But we're not accustomed to ruling on our own. The people... they need guidance."

Red Mist's eyes narrowed slightly. "That guidance should not come from another person who seeks to dominate. It should come from within your community. The temple will offer wisdom. Don't make the same mistake twice."

The elder nodded again, though Red Mist could sense his hesitation. The weight of the town's future was already settling on him, and she knew the temptation of power would loom over them all in the coming days. But it wasn't her place to intervene further.

As they turned to leave, Wakamono cast one last glance over his shoulder at the elders, watching as they huddled together, whispering about what should be done next. He felt a strange mixture of hope and unease. "Do you think they'll make the right choices?" he asked, his voice soft, almost hopeful.

Red Mist shook her head slightly. "I don't know," she admitted, her tone weary. "People often repeat their mistakes. Someone will rise up, eventually. Someone with ambition, hunger for power."

Wakamono frowned, a knot forming in his chest. "But we saved them," he said. "We gave them a chance to be free."

Red Mist stopped walking for a moment, turning to face him, her expression serious. "Freedom isn't just something you hand over, Wakamono. It's something people have to fight for, every day. We've done what we can, but the rest is up to them. We can't control their future, and we shouldn't try to."

Wakamono nodded slowly, absorbing her words. It wasn't the ending he had hoped for. He had imagined the people celebrating, grateful for their freedom, but reality was far more complicated than he'd realized. He felt the weight of the lessons he had learned in Hanamachi pressing down on him.

Red Mist placed a hand on his shoulder. "We've done our duty here," she said softly. "Now, we move on."

As they continued their journey out of the town, the sun rose higher in the sky, casting long shadows over the streets. The sound of distant murmurs from the town elders echoed behind them, but Red Mist didn't look back. She knew that Hanamachi's future was uncertain, but it was no longer her concern.

Wakamono, on the other hand, couldn't shake the feeling that they had left something unfinished. He glanced at Red Mist, who walked beside him with her usual calm, and wondered how she carried the weight of such responsibilities with such grace.

"Do you think... we'll ever come back here?" he asked, his voice tentative.

Red Mist's gaze remained fixed on the path ahead. "If we do," she said, "I hope it's not because the town has fallen into the hands of another tyrant."

Wakamono fell silent, contemplating her words as they walked away from the town that had once been prosperous but now stood on the precipice of an uncertain future.

後見

As Red Mist and Wakamono made their way along the narrow mountain path, the morning sun was abruptly swallowed by thick, churning clouds. The air around them grew cold and heavy, the brightness of the sky fading into an eerie twilight. Wakamono paused, glancing up at the sudden shift in the atmosphere, a deep unease settling in his gut.

"Red Mist," he said quietly, his eyes scanning the horizon. "Do you see that?"

Red Mist, already alert, stopped beside him, her hand instinctively resting on the hilt of her katana. She looked up at the swirling clouds, her sharp eyes narrowing as the wind picked up, rustling the leaves and kicking up dust along the path. The sky above Hanamachi was darkening at an unnatural speed, thick, black clouds spiraling as if being drawn to a point just above the town.

Before they could take another step, a shrill, bone-chilling screech pierced the air. It echoed through the valley, sending flocks of birds scattering from the treetops in fear. The sound was unlike anything Wakamono had ever heard, and his heart pounded in his chest as he gripped the hilt of his own blade.

"What... what is that?" Wakamono muttered, his voice tight.

Red Mist didn't answer immediately. Her eyes remained fixed on the distant town as the clouds coalesced into a single, dense mass overhead. The wind howled through the trees, and then, from the heart of the storm, something massive and winged descended from the sky.

The creature's form was both monstrous and awe-inspiring. It moved with the grace of a predator, its massive, blackened wings flapping with the force of a gale as it swooped low over the town. Its body was covered in bristling black fur, matted and thick, and its face was a grotesque, snarling visage with the eyes of a feral beast. Flames licked the tips of its sharp, jagged teeth, and the faint glow of fire burned in the slits of its catlike eyes.

Wakamono's breath caught in his throat. "Is that a...?"

"A kasha," Red Mist said grimly, her voice steady despite the ominous sight before them. "A corpse-stealer."

As the kasha swooped lower, the townspeople scattered in terror, running for cover as its shadow passed over the streets. It circled once before diving sharply toward the estate, where Shiro's body lay, bloodied and broken.

The kasha's claws extended, massive talons glowing faintly with the heat of the creature's internal fire. In one fluid motion, it seized Shiro's lifeless corpse from the ground, lifting him with ease. The villagers, many of them too shocked to scream, watched in horror as the kasha rose high into the sky, Shiro's body hanging limp in its grasp.

Wakamono's blood ran cold as he watched the creature soar into the darkened sky. "Why would it take him?" he asked, his voice barely above a whisper.

Red Mist's gaze remained on the kasha as it ascended, the fire in its eyes glowing brighter with each passing second. "The kasha feeds on the souls of the wicked," she said softly, her voice carrying a weight of ancient knowledge. "It takes those who have strayed too far toward malevolence, evil. Shiro's soul... was already lost."

They stood in silence for a moment, watching as the kasha vanished into the storm, the clouds swirling in its wake. Thunder rumbled in the distance, and the sky remained shrouded in darkness, a chilling reminder of what had just transpired.

Wakamono exhaled slowly, his mind reeling from the sight of the creature. "I... I didn't know those actually existed."

"There is much you don't know yet," Red Mist replied, turning her gaze back toward the mountain pass. "The kasha is a rare sight, but its presence is a warning. We should move quickly."

As they continued their journey, the dark clouds lingered over Hanamachi, casting long shadows over the town and its people. Wakamono couldn't shake the image of the kasha, its fiery eyes and monstrous form seared into his memory. Shiro's fate had been sealed, but the darkness that hung over the town now felt more palpable, more threatening than ever before.

Red Mist remained silent beside him, but Wakamono could sense the unease in her posture, the tension in her movements. The kasha had not only taken Shiro's body—it had left a chilling reminder of the power of the forces that lay beyond his understanding.

後見

The wind howled through the narrow mountain pass, tugging at the cloaks of Red Mist and Wakamono as they made their way along the treacherous path. The sky overhead remained ominous, dark clouds hanging low, casting long shadows over the craggy rocks.

Red Mist was leading the way, her movements fluid and controlled as always. But even she seemed tense, her eyes scanning the cliffs and treeline for any signs of danger.

"We'll be clear of the mountains soon," Red Mist said, her voice barely audible over the wind.

Wakamono nodded, though his unease only grew. There was something in the air—something that felt wrong. He couldn't shake the feeling that they were being watched.

Suddenly, a guttural roar echoed off the cliffs, freezing them both in place. Wakamono's hand instinctively went to his katana, his heart racing as he turned toward the source of the sound. From the shadows of the forest, three hulking figures emerged—oni, their towering forms bristling with muscle and malice.

The lead oni snarled, brandishing a massive iron club, its red eyes gleaming with bloodlust. The two behind him were just as fearsome, their twisted faces contorted in savage grins, tusks protruding from their lower jaws.

"Stay close," Red Mist muttered, drawing her katana with a deadly calm.

The oni moved with terrifying speed, closing the distance between them in seconds. Wakamono's heart pounded in his chest as he stood his ground, drawing his blade and positioning himself beside Red Mist.

The lead oni swung its club with a ferocious roar, the force of the blow cracking the ground where they stood. Red Mist ducked beneath the strike, her katana flashing as she countered with a precise slash across the oni's arm. But the creature barely flinched, its thick skin and monstrous strength making it a formidable opponent.

Wakamono parried a blow from the second oni, but the impact nearly knocked him off his feet, sending him stumbling back toward the edge of the cliff. He could hear the rocks crumbling beneath his feet, the sheer drop just inches behind him. Fear gripped his chest as the oni advanced, its cruel eyes locking onto him.

"Red Mist!" Wakamono shouted, desperation creeping into his voice as he was forced back.

The third oni let out a thunderous roar, moving to flank them, cutting off their retreat. Red Mist, locked in battle with the lead oni, couldn't break away to help. For a moment, it seemed like they were trapped, backed against the edge of the cliff with no escape.

Suddenly, from the treeline behind the oni, a new sound erupted—a crashing, primal bellow. Before Wakamono could even process what was happening, a massive figure charged out of the trees, barreling into the nearest oni with the force of an avalanche.

It was a hibagon.

The beast slammed into the oni, knocking it clean off the edge of the cliff with a single, brutal strike. The oni let out a startled scream as it plummeted into the abyss below, disappearing from sight.

The remaining two oni turned, momentarily stunned by the unexpected appearance of the hibagon. The beast let out a ferocious roar, its wild eyes gleaming with fury as it squared off against the second oni. Without hesitation, the hibagon lunged at the creature, its powerful arms swinging in savage arcs as the two monsters clashed in a chaotic brawl.

Red Mist seized the opportunity, her katana flashing in the dim light as she pressed the attack on the lead oni. Wakamono, regaining his footing, rushed to her side, his blade meeting the oni's club with a sharp clash of steel. Together, they fought with precision and skill, slowly wearing down their foe.

The battle raged on, the sound of steel against flesh and the thunderous roars of the hibagon and oni echoing off the cliffs. Wakamono ducked beneath a wild swing from the oni's club, countering with a quick slash across its leg. The creature howled in pain, staggering back, but still refused to fall.

Meanwhile, the hibagon was locked in a savage duel with the remaining oni, the two beasts tearing into each other with raw, brutal force. Trees snapped like twigs as they crashed through the forest, their roars shaking the very ground beneath them.

Finally, with a well-timed strike, Red Mist drove her katana deep into the lead oni's chest. The creature let out a final, strangled roar before collapsing to the ground, its body thudding heavily against the rocks.

Breathing hard, Wakamono turned just in time to see the hibagon deliver a bone-crushing blow to the second oni, sending it careening into a nearby boulder. The creature slumped to the ground, defeated.

The hibagon, panting and bloodied, stood over its fallen foe for a moment, its wild eyes scanning the battlefield. Then, without a word or a glance toward Red Mist or Wakamono, it turned and lumbered back into the forest, vanishing into the shadows as quickly as it had appeared.

Wakamono stared after it, his mind reeling from the encounter. "Was that...?"

"Yes," Red Mist said quietly, her gaze following the hibagon's retreating form. "The same one."

Wakamono had noticed the scars that marked the hibagon's body, the wounds from their first battle still visible beneath its thick fur. The creature had shown no gratitude, no acknowledgment of the mercy they had shown it. And yet, it had come to their aid in their moment of need.

"Why did it help us?" Wakamono asked, sheathing his katana with a frown.

Red Mist wiped the blood from her blade, her expression thoughtful. "Some bonds are formed in ways we can't understand. Perhaps it remembered what we did for it. Or perhaps it simply saw the oni as a threat to its territory."

Wakamono nodded slowly, though the weight of the encounter lingered in his mind. The path of the Kōken was never as simple as it seemed. The lines between friend and foe, mercy and violence, were more blurred now than ever.

With a final glance at the cliff's edge, Red Mist gestured for them to continue. "Come. The pass is still long, and the day grows short."

As they moved deeper into the mountain pass, Wakamono couldn't help but feel that the battle had been more than just a random encounter. Something larger was at play, forces beyond their control weaving their fates together in ways they couldn't yet see.

And with Shiro's fall and the dark clouds still hanging over Hanamachi, he had a feeling the worst was yet to come.

11
十一

THE AIR IN SANPUKU City was crisp as the early morning sun bathed the training courtyard in soft light. Wakamono and Red Mist stood in the center, both breathing steadily after an intense session of combat forms. Wakamono wiped the sweat from his brow, his mind still racing from their recent experiences. It felt good to be back in the familiar surroundings of the mountain city, where the world seemed less chaotic, and life was simpler. But the questions in his mind refused to settle.

Red Mist, as always, seemed composed, her movements precise and unyielding even after the grueling training. She adjusted the grip on her katana, her expression calm, though Wakamono sensed a certain tension behind her quiet demeanor.

Wakamono paused for a moment, his curiosity bubbling to the surface. The battle with Shiro had left so many questions unanswered. He couldn't help but wonder what their past had been like, the bond that Red Mist and Shiro once shared.

He sheathed his katana and glanced toward Red Mist. "Sensei," he began hesitantly, "I've been thinking... about Shiro."

Red Mist's eyes flicked toward him, but she said nothing, her focus still on the blade in her hands.

Wakamono pressed on. "What was he like? When you were both apprentices, I mean. You two must have been close."

Red Mist's movements stilled. She didn't answer immediately, her gaze drifting to the distant mountains. For a long moment, Wakamono thought she wouldn't respond at all, but then she exhaled slowly and spoke, her voice measured.

"Shiro was talented," she said, her tone cool. "He had passion, strength, and a sharp mind. But he was always restless—always looking for more than what our master was willing to teach."

Wakamono frowned. "Restless? You mean he wasn't satisfied with the Kōken training?"

"He wasn't satisfied with anything," Red Mist replied, her eyes narrowing slightly as the memories seemed to resurface. "Shiro sought power. He thought that the world wasn't fit to govern itself, and he believed that our path as Kōken was... limiting. At the time, it was something I foolishly admired."

There was a note of bitterness in her voice that Wakamono hadn't heard before. It was clear that her memories of Shiro were still raw, even after all this time. Wakamono shifted, unsure of how to proceed.

"So… you two weren't close, then?" he asked, carefully.

Red Mist's gaze turned hard. "We were rivals. Our master made sure of that."

Wakamono blinked, surprised by the sudden sharpness in her words. He had never seen this side of Red Mist before. The stoic, calm demeanor she always maintained seemed to crack slightly as she spoke of the past.

"Our master… he believed that the best way to train us was through competition," she continued, her voice dropping. "Every day was a test. A challenge. He pit us against each other, pushed us to our limits, made us fight for every scrap of approval. It wasn't training—it was survival."

Wakamono remained silent, sensing that this was not an easy topic for her. He had never imagined that Red Mist's journey had been so harsh. He had only ever seen her as a master of discipline and self-control, but hearing about her own struggles as an apprentice gave him a new perspective.

"What was he like?" Wakamono asked, unable to stop himself. "Your master, I mean."

Red Mist's expression darkened, her lips pressing into a thin line. "Cruel," she said simply. "He was a harsh disciplinarian, more focused on results than on teaching. Every mistake was met with punishment, every success with indifference."

Wakamono stared at her, trying to imagine what it must have been like to train under such a master. It seemed so different from the way Red Mist had trained him—with guidance, patience, and understanding.

"He never showed any humor," Red Mist added quietly. "He didn't believe in it. To him, the world was a place of suffering and conflict, and he believed that we needed to be forged in that fire if we were to survive."

The weight of her words hung in the air, and Wakamono found himself at a loss for what to say. He had always respected Red Mist for her strength and wisdom, but now, knowing what she had endured to become the Kōken she was today, that respect deepened even further.

"Sensei... I didn't know," Wakamono said softly.

Red Mist shook her head. "There's no need for sympathy, Wakamono. The past is behind me, and I have learned from it."

She turned to face him fully, her eyes sharp but calm. "As for Shiro... I will not speak of him any further. What he became, the path he chose, is his alone. He was not the man I once knew, and his absolute betrayal of the Kōken ideals is unforgivable."

Wakamono nodded, understanding the pain in her voice. "I understand."

Red Mist let out a slow breath, as if releasing the memories she had just dredged up. "We will continue to train, but not now. Not today. There is much to reflect on."

She paused, her gaze softening slightly as she looked at him. "In time, I will tell you more about my master. But not today."

Wakamono bowed his head in respect, feeling the weight of her words. "Thank you, sensei."

Red Mist gestured toward the mountains in the distance, the sky beginning to take on the golden hue of late afternoon. "For now, let us return to quiet reflection."

Wakamono followed her gaze, the sun casting long shadows over the city below. As they stood in silence, the gravity of their journey and the battles they had fought lingered between them, a shared understanding of the burdens they both carried.

The road ahead was still long, and there were many more lessons to learn.

END

終

Epilogue

THE AIR IN THE cave was thick with the scent of decay and smoke, the constant crackling of burning herbs filling the dim, stifling space. The mountain cave, perched high above the treacherous paths below, was a place few dared to tread. The walls, jagged and blackened, were lined with ancient talismans and decayed remnants of offerings from long-forgotten villagers. The flickering light from the dying embers in the center of the cave cast shadows that danced wildly across the floor, twisting into grotesque forms.

At the heart of the cave, hunched over a cauldron of boiling liquid, was Yama-uba herself. Her once human face had long since withered into something monstrous—pale, cracked skin stretched tight over sunken bones, and eyes that gleamed with a malevolent madness. Her tattered robes dragged along the ground as she moved, her thin lips muttering incomprehensible nonsense as she stirred the pot. Her gnarled fingers clawed at the air, as if grasping at invisible threads of some intricate, sinister plan only she could see.

"They took it from me... took it from me... foolish child..." she muttered, her voice raspy, broken by fits of manic laughter. "Shiro... Shiro thought he was strong... but he was weak... too weak... yes... yes... too weak for the blade... wasted faith... wasted visions."

A gust of icy wind swept through the cave, but Yama-uba paid it no mind. Her eyes were wild, darting back and forth, seeing things only her fractured mind could comprehend. Her focus shifted between the boiling cauldron and the shadows that gathered at the cave's edge.

Three figures emerged from those shadows, their towering forms filling the cave with an overwhelming sense of dread. The akuma—demons forged from the darkest corners of the spirit world—had arrived.

Each akuma was more monstrous than the last, their forms embodying different aspects of malevolence. The first, broad and hunched, was covered in jagged, charred scales, its massive arms ending in claws that seemed to drip with corrosive black ooze. Its eyes burned with hatred, and every step it took left deep, smoldering imprints in the ground.

The second was a twisting mass of sinewy tendrils and limbs, its form constantly shifting, as if it could not decide whether to walk as a beast or slither as a serpent. Its skin was pale and sickly, and where its face should have been, there was only an empty void that emanated a low, droning hum that caused the air to thrum with unease.

The third akuma was the most terrifying of all—a figure cloaked in swirling shadows, with long, elegant horns spiraling from its head. Its face was obscured, save for two glowing red eyes that peered out from the darkness like fiery embers. It radiated an aura of cold calculation and malice, the embodiment of sinister intelligence.

Yama-uba cackled gleefully as the akuma approached, their presence filling the cave with an oppressive weight. She danced around the cauldron, her twisted form moving with a grotesque, unnatural grace.

"Shiro failed me," she hissed, pointing a crooked finger at the shadows as if they were responsible for his failure. "He was a fool! A greedy, prideful fool! Couldn't see past his own desires... yes... wasted, wasted... all wasted... but he will serve again."

Her laughter rang through the cave, echoing off the walls like the wail of a banshee. The akuma watched her with silent, sinister patience, their forms unmoving as Yama-uba ranted and raved. They had no need for haste. They knew that they were inevitable, their power unmatched in the mortal realm.

The first akuma, the charred and hulking brute, stepped forward, its voice a low rumble that vibrated the very air. "The oni failed as well."

Yama-uba waved her hand dismissively, a sneer curling her cracked lips. "The oni were feeble fools! Brainless cretins! But the boy..." Her eyes gleamed. "The boy and the blade... yes... the blade...."

Her voice lowered to a whisper, and she began pacing, her feet dragging across the cave floor as she muttered. "The healing blade... it must be mine... I saw it in the boy's hand... felt its power... it heals, yes, but it can do more... it can undo...."

The second akuma, the writhing mass of tendrils, let out a rasping hiss. "And what would you have us do, witch?"

Yama-uba stopped her pacing, her bony hands raised toward the dark heavens as if beseeching the very spirits themselves. "Find the blade! Bring it to me! With that power, I can reshape the world... death will bend to me... I will rewrite the fates themselves!"

The third akuma, the shadowy figure with the piercing red eyes, stepped forward, its voice like the hiss of a blade sliding from its sheath. "The blade is in the hands of the Kōken. It will not be easy to retrieve."

Yama-uba turned her wild gaze to the demon, a mad smile twisting her face. "Easy? No, no... nothing is easy... but I see the paths, I see the future... the boy will falter, yes... and when he does, the blade will be mine...."

She let out another cackle, spinning in place as if the victory was already hers. "The Kōken think they can protect the world... but they will fall, one by one... and when they are gone, I will have the blade!"

The akuma remained silent, their dark forms radiating malice and power as Yama-uba's voice grew softer, more cryptic. "The blade... the key to... it can bring life... but it can also take it away... Shiro was too blind to see... too selfish... but I...."

She trailed off, her eyes glazing over as her mind wandered to unseen places. The akuma exchanged glances, their expressions unreadable, but their purpose clear. The blade had to be found, and its power brought under their control.

With one last mad giggle, Yama-uba waved her hand toward the akuma, dismissing them. "Go, go... find it... find the blade... bring it to me... we have much to do...."

The akuma turned and melted back into the shadows, their forms dissolving into the darkness of the cave. Yama-uba stood alone once more, her eyes gleaming with malevolent glee as she muttered to herself, the plans of darkness spinning in her broken mind.

As the last of the akuma vanished, Yama-uba's voice echoed through the cave, a whispered promise that carried the weight of ancient power.

"Soon... very soon...."

www.ingramcontent.com/pod-product-compliance
Lightning Source LLC
Chambersburg PA
CBHW022120170626
46808CB00002B/787